Lights, Camera, COOK!

NEXT BEST JUNIOR CHEF

EPISODE 1

Lights, Camera, COOK!

by **Charise Mericle Harper**

with illustrations by **Aurélie Blard-Quintard**

HOUGHTON MIFFLIN HARCOURT
Boston   New York

hmhco.com

The text was set in Garamond Premier Pro.
Illustrations by Aurélie Blard-Quintard
Illustrations by Andrea Miller, pages 174–78

The Library of Congress has cataloged the hardcover edition as follows:
Names: Harper, Charise Mericle, author. | Blard-Quintard, Aurélie,
illustrator.
Title: Lights, camera, cook! / Charise Mericle Harper ; illustrated by
Aurélie Blard-Quintard.
Description: Boston ; New York : HMH Books for Young Readers, 2017. | Series:
Next Best Junior Chef ; 1 | Summary: Follows Tate, Rae, Caroline, and
Oliver, ages nine to twelve, both on and off camera as they compete in a
televised cooking competition. Includes cooking tips.
Identifiers: LCCN 2016038369
Subjects: | CYAC: Cooking—Fiction. | Contests—Fiction. |
Television—Production and direction—Fiction. | Friendship—Fiction. |
BISAC: JUVENILE FICTION / Cooking & Food. | JUVENILE FICTION / Action &
Adventure / General. | JUVENILE FICTION / Humorous Stories. | JUVENILE
FICTION / Performing Arts / Television & Radio. | JUVENILE FICTION / Media
Tie-In. | JUVENILE FICTION / Business, Careers, Occupations.
Classification: LCC PZ7.H231323 Lig 2017 | DDC [Fic]—dc23
LC record available at https://lccn.loc.gov/2016038369

ISBN: 978-0-544-91260-1 paper over board
ISBN: 978-1-328-50701-3 paperback

Printed in the United States of America
DOC 10 9 8 7 6 5 4 3 2 1

4500715932

Thank you to my mother, for always making a home-cooked meal.

Thank you to Ruth Oliver, for support and cooking tips.

Thank you to Frances Smith, for helping bring Oliver to life.

Thank you to the food trucks of Portland, because who has time to cook and write?

CHAPTER 1

The filming studio was a hive of activity. And then . . .

"BOOMS!"

"LIGHTS!"

"CAMERAS!"

"ROLLING!"

There was silence. Everyone waited.

"Welcome to *Next Best Junior Chef,* where all the action is in the kitchen!" The announcer's voice filled the air with energy and excitement. "This week, four young chefs will battle it out in a series of challenges that will test their culinary skills, knowledge, and creativity. Thursday's challenge will send one chef home, and the three remaining contestants will be one step closer to the final elimination round. Pick your favorites now, because one of these talented chefs WILL BE the Next Best Junior Chef!

"Our esteemed judges include Chef Vera Porter of the famous Porter Farm Restaurant, renowned pastry chef Aimee

1

Copley, and Chef Gary Lee, restaurant proprietor and host of the award-winning show *Adventures in Cooking*. Make no mistake, the judges will be watching our competitors very closely. Everything counts, and will be taken into consideration, when we get to the final elimination round.

"Our young chefs will be mentored by Chef Nancy Patel, the 2013 recipient of the Golden Spoon Award.

"The winner of *Next Best Junior Chef* will receive two life-changing prizes: a food truck specially designed for the winner *and* a guest spot on *Adventures in Cooking* when it begins filming this summer in . . . the beautiful countryside of Italy!

"Our four young chefs have survived countless interviews, taste tests, and chopping challenges. They can purée, sauté, broil, bake, and fry with skill beyond their years. They're the cream of the crop, and they can't wait to get cooking. So, let's meet our competitors."

The junior chefs were lined up and ready outside the big doorway of the filming studio. As soon as the announcer called their names, they'd come in, one at a time, for a grand entrance. Chef Nancy had prepared them, because once the cameras were rolling, everything had to be perfect.

The announcer continued: "*Next Best Junior Chef* invites contestant Caroline to the table. Caroline is from Chicago, Illinois."

Chef Nancy tapped Caroline on the shoulder. "Go."

Caroline took a deep breath and walked through the door and down the ramp toward the front of the room. She passed the workstations, one of which would be hers, but she didn't look. Her eyes stayed glued to her destination. The judges, Chef Gary, Chef Aimee, and Chef Porter, stood next to one another behind a long table, smiling and waiting.

Chef Gary stepped forward. "Welcome, Caroline. Please tell us: How did you get to be such a good cook?"

The cameras, the lights, the judges—these made Caroline nervous, but not the question. She knew exactly what to say. Chef Nancy had helped them practice their answers.

"I'm lucky—I've been around good food my whole life. My family owns a French bistro and my mother is a chef, so I speak French, English, and food. It's like a third language for me. Cooking is a way to express myself."

"Wow!" Chef Gary took a step back. "How old are you?"

"Eleven."

"Well, I can't wait to see what your food is going to tell us."

Caroline blushed. "Thank you, Chef."

The interview was over. Tate was next. Caroline breathed a sigh of relief.

"*Next Best Junior Chef* invites contestant Tate to the table. Tate hails from Seattle, Washington."

Tate couldn't wait to get to the front of the room. It was hard not to run, and then when he got there, it was hard to stand still.

Chef Aimee smiled and leaned forward. "Welcome, Tate—I know I'm supposed to ask you a cooking question, but first I have to know . . . how old are you?"

Tate swayed back and forth on the balls of his feet. "Nine."

Chef Aimee shook her head. "Unbelievable! You're our

youngest contestant ever. Congratulations! Was it difficult to become one of the four junior chefs in this competition?"

Tate chopped the air with his hand. "Not really. I'm good with a knife, and I like cooking, so it was fun. People are always surprised when they see what I can do in the kitchen."

Chef Aimee smiled. "Ooh, I like surprises. Well done, Tate. I can't wait for you to surprise me, too."

Tate nodded and grinned until he heard the announcer's voice.

"*Next Best Junior Chef* invites contestant Oliver to the—"

"CUT! CUT! CUT!" A man brushed past Oliver and ran down the ramp. "Take five! Camera problem. We'll start up again in five minutes tops."

Chef Nancy called Oliver back from the ramp. "I'm sorry, Oliver. We'll start again when Steve gives us the signal. He's the producer, so if he says it's only five minutes, I'm sure he's right."

Oliver nodded. "Yes, ma'am." He could wait. He was the King of Calm.

CHAPTER 2

liver timed the break. It was four minutes and fifty-three seconds—less than five minutes. Steve was right. Oliver smiled. He liked precision, things in order—no surprises. He took his place at the door and waited for the announcer.

"*Next Best Junior Chef* invites contestant Oliver to the table. Oliver is twelve and from Montgomery, Alabama."

Oliver marched down the ramp, his shoulders back and head high. He'd practiced at home in front of the mirror. First impressions were important—that's what his mom said, and he believed her. She was good with image stuff; she was a designer.

When he got to the front he looked right at Chef Porter. You could learn a lot from paying attention. The judges were going down the line, taking turns with the questions. He smiled, feeling lucky. His question was coming from the best chef there.

Chef Porter smiled back. "Welcome, Oliver. Can you tell us what excites you most about this competition?"

Oliver waited for a second and then answered. The King of Calm did not rush. "Yes, ma'am. I'm excited about the opportunity to learn new things, and then use that knowledge to refine my cooking skills. Being a chef is a journey, not a destination. I want my food to reflect my journey of discovery and excitement, but in a quiet, thoughtful way. In the kitchen, I am the King of Calm."

Chef Porter clasped her hands over her heart. "Well said, Oliver. I look forward to seeing the fruits of that journey."

Rae was the last contestant, but she didn't mind. It was better than going first. Last gave you time to absorb the details, notice things. She'd listened to Oliver's answer but she had no idea what he was talking about. "Journey," "discovery," "king"—it was all a jumble. And then the announcer was calling her name.

"And last but certainly not least, *Next Best Junior Chef* invites contestant Rae to the table. Rae is eleven years old and from Port Chester, New York."

Steve nodded to Chef Nancy and she tapped Rae on the shoulder. "Go."

Rae stepped through the door. Everything was brighter than she'd imagined, and blurry. Like a dream—out of focus. She moved slowly down the ramp toward the front of the room. It took longer than it had in the practice, but finally she was there, next to Oliver.

"Welcome, Rae—so happy you are with us." Chef Gary's

face was swirling, his voice distant, and then . . . everything went dark.

Chef Nancy rushed forward, but she wouldn't make it. Rae was already falling—in a second she'd be on the ground. And then two arms shot out and caught her. It was a surprise, lucky and unexpected. It was Oliver.

Oliver hadn't even thought about it. It was just a reflex. Playing catch was his favorite pastime—after cooking, of course—and he was good at it. In the battle against gravity, Oliver always won. Rae was slumped in his arms, heavy. He almost dropped her, but then there was help. The medics, the judges, and Chef Nancy, suddenly everyone was there.

CHAPTER 3

Rae was sitting up, talking, sipping water. She was going to be fine. Chef Nancy gave everyone a thirty-minute break while the studio staff figured out what to do next. Steve the producer and a cameraperson got some reactions while they waited. Tate was happy for the chance to move around.

CAROLINE

I was smiling at Rae while she was walking down the ramp, because girls need to stick together. We're not friends yet, but we will be. I can just tell. The fainting was scary. I'm glad she's okay. She's lucky Oliver was there to catch her. I know this is a competition, but I like that we can still help each other.

Oliver's a hero. He saved Rae! That's the kind of thing my dad does in the army. He saves people all over the world. First he was in Afghanistan, and now he's in South Korea. It's really hard to have him be so far away, but he's brave, so I can be brave too.

TATE

OLIVER

No, sir, I do not think I'm a hero. When I see something that needs to be done, I just do it. I'm glad Rae is okay and glad that I could help.

A contestant fainting in front of the judges was something new. It was a shock to everyone. Usually the producer didn't like surprises, but this was different. It was the kind of twist that made him smile. The King of Calm saving a fellow contestant was perfect for TV.

Steve was ecstatic. "Audiences love a hero!"

After a short meeting with Chef Nancy, Steve gave her a new job—making sure Oliver lived up to his name.

When Rae was recovered, everyone lined up in front of the judges again so she could film her interview.

Steve held up his hand. "Rolling!"

That was the word that got everything started. The cameras turned on.

Chef Gary gently shook Rae's hand. "Welcome, Rae—so happy you're okay. That was quite a fall. I don't usually get that kind of reaction from a new contestant."

Rae blushed and looked down. "Well, I was really excited and I guess I didn't drink enough water, and . . . I got kind of dizzy."

Chef Gary feigned disbelief. "WHAT? So it wasn't that you were in awe of me because I'm a rock star of cooking?"

Chef Aimee leaned over and interrupted. "You might be a cooking star, but you're no rock star." She covered her ears. "You do not want to hear this man sing."

Everyone laughed.

Chef Gary held up his hand. "Wait a minute. Are you daring me to sing? Because an Adventure Chef never says no to a . . ." Chef Gary pointed to the contestants.

"CHALLENGE!" they all shouted together.

They all knew what to say. It was Chef Gary's famous tag line from his other show, *Adventures in Cooking.*

Chef Porter clapped her hands. Once, twice—the whole room went silent. She had that kind of power. "I'm going to step in here so we can talk about something other than Chef Gary's singing."

Chef Gary made a face like his feelings were hurt, but Chef Porter ignored him.

She smiled at Rae. "Rae, can you tell us . . . was there someone in your life who encouraged you to cook?"

Rae nodded. "My grandma, she loves watching cooking shows on TV. We'd watch them all the time, and then one day we just decided to try some of the recipes. Pretty soon we were cooking new things almost every day. And then when our neighbors found out, they gave us even more recipes to try."

"What dish are you most proud of?" asked Chef Aimee.

Rae smiled. This was the exact question she was expecting. "Baklava. It's a dessert from Turkey, with honey, pistachios, and walnuts. It takes hours to make, and the filo dough is really tricky. You have to be really careful with it or it'll all stick together in a big doughy clump."

"I know it." Chef Aimee shook her head. "Not an easy dish to make, but certainly an easy one to eat!" She patted her tummy. "Congratulations and welcome. I can't wait to see the new recipes you'll try out on us."

"Thank you, Chef." Rae smiled and double nodded. Once for the compliment and once because the interview was over. She exhaled a sigh of relief.

But the relief didn't last long. There were more interviews, for all of them. Chef Nancy pointed to a row of stools on the other side of the filming studio.

"You'll be doing regular interviews with Steve. We need them for TV, but don't be nervous, Steve will guide you—it'll be fun and easy."

When they got to the stools, Steve introduced Janet and Mark, two camerapeople. They looked up, waved, and then disappeared behind their cameras again.

Steve pointed to the stools. "Okay, chefs. Please take a seat." When everyone was seated he continued. "If we do this right, it won't take long. There are only two things to remember." He held up a finger. "Number one—always answer honestly, and number two . . ." He added another finger. "When I ask you a question, please repeat the question first before giving your answer. For example, if I ask: *Why do you like apples?*, you say: *I like apples because* . . . and then you tell me your answer. Does everyone understand?"

Four heads bobbed up and down.

"Super!" Steve high-fived the air. "Okay, let's get started. Today's question is . . . Why will you be the Next Best Junior Chef?"

I will be the Next Best Junior Chef because I have a good understanding of all the skills involved in cooking. I know how different foods and spices work together.

CAROLINE

OLIVER

I will be the Next Best Junior Chef because I'm cool, *calm*, creative, and collected. I think things through and I never make mistakes.

I will be the Next Best Junior Chef because I'm excited about cooking and I'm not afraid to try new things.

RAE

TATE

I will be the Next Best Junior Chef because I'm an inventor. I like creating interesting food combinations people have never tasted before.

CHAPTER 4

orter Farm was impressively large. In addition to the filming complex, it supported a working farm, a world-class restaurant, a residential lodge, and acres of natural wooded forest. After a picnic lunch, Chef Nancy took the junior chefs on a tour of the facilities.

Caroline looked around and then breathed a sigh of relief. "No cameras."

Rae nodded. She felt exactly the same.

The first stop was the filming studio, where they'd originally met the judges. Everyone wanted to know the same thing: which workstation would be theirs for the competition. The four workstations were identical. Each had a stove, a sink, an oven, and a folded apron sitting in the middle of the table. The only difference was the embroidered name on the front of the apron.

Caroline ran her finger over the smooth bumps in her name.

"Remember," said Chef Nancy, "please don't move anything. These stations are set up for the competition. You can explore later when we're working in the school studio."

Caroline pulled her hand back and glued it to her side. Chef Nancy had eagle eyes.

Chef Nancy gave Caroline a mini-nod and then continued. "There's a wide assortment of tools for you to use, right at your own workstation. And don't worry, everyone has the same thing: mixers, food processors, knives, and so on."

Chef Nancy pointed to the front of the room. "Next stop, the pantry." It was to the left, behind the big table where they'd met the judges. The fruits and vegetables were stacked in bins in the middle of the room like an island—the vegetables on one side, the fruits on the other.

Chef Nancy held up a mushroom. "Morels, enoki, and chanterelles. We stock a wide variety of high-end ingredients for you to use."

Oliver turned away. He wasn't a fan. He'd only use the mushrooms if he absolutely had to.

Chef Nancy pointed to the three big refrigerator doors at the end of the room. "There's one for dairy, one for sauces and specialty items, and this last one's a freezer." Her phone buzzed and she looked down at the screen. "Oops, we're behind schedule. Time to move on."

Chef Nancy led the way out of the filming studio and into a hallway. She stopped in front of a big red door and pushed it open.

"This is the school studio. We'll have some of our cooking lessons in here, when we aren't filming with the judges. The worktables are set up exactly like the ones in the filming studio. This is on purpose, so you can be comfortable and familiar with your workspaces. You'll have lots of time to look around tomorrow. No one wants to use up competition time looking for a spatula."

It was a joke, but no one laughed. They were all thinking the same thing: *I hope that doesn't happen to me.*

Chef Nancy closed the door. "Next stop: the recipe library."

OLIVER

My least favorite ingredient? I don't have one. I like everything. A good chef knows that all ingredients are unique and important. The Next Best Junior Chef has to be open to anything.

The library was impressive. Two walls with floor-to-ceiling books flanked a large picture window overlooking a small pond. Several comfy-looking sofas and a long table surrounded by chairs filled the center of the room.

Chef Nancy pointed to one of the book ladders. "You're welcome to come in here and study recipes in your free time, but please be careful if you're climbing."

The library's amazing. I've never seen so many cookbooks in my entire life! I personally only own two cookbooks. There must be thousands in there, from all over the world. It's really a chef's dream come true!

RAE

Chef Nancy hurried the group down a walkway and out two big black doors. The view was spectacular: green hills framed the distant sky and a cobblestone path led to a large log building. Porter Lodge was the last stop on the tour. It's

where the kids would eat, sleep, and relax when they weren't on camera.

Chef Nancy pointed to the lodge. "Your rooms are ready. Go look, explore. You don't have to wait for me."

Everyone ran ahead, except Oliver. He stayed with Chef Nancy all the way to the door, which of course he held open.

"Oh, how thoughtful. Thank you." Chef Nancy seemed surprised.

Oliver nodded and smiled. Cool, calm, and a gentleman. He was going to win this thing.

CHAPTER 5

hef Nancy had a speech, and when everyone was seated at the big table eating breakfast, she started. "Welcome to day one of the *Next Best Junior Chef* challenges! I know you're excited and can't wait to get started, but before we begin, I want to go over a few things. Number one: the cameras."

That got everyone's attention. Oliver looked up, Tate dropped his toast, Caroline put down her spoon, and Rae stopped chewing.

"Some of you might be nervous about the filming, but don't be. We're not asking you to bite off more than you can chew. You'll get used to the cameras, I promise. Before long, you won't even notice they're there."

Caroline shook her head, leaned toward Rae, and whispered: "Do you think a person can be allergic to cameras?" She scratched her arm. "They make me itchy. Plus, what if I make a mistake? It'll be on TV. The whole world will see it!"

Rae nodded, but Caroline couldn't tell if she was agreeing with the worry or the allergy part.

Chef Nancy continued. "Being on TV is exciting, but I want you to remember, you're chefs, not actors. It might be tempting to show off for the cameras, but save that energy for your cooking! You're going to need it. We have a busy schedule. There are mini-challenges today, tomorrow, and Monday; a field trip challenge on Tuesday; and the first elimination challenge on Thursday." Chef Nancy handed out a paper with the schedule of events. "This is going to be an exciting week. Are you ready for fun?"

CONFIDENTIAL!
Schedule of Events for
Week One (Episode One)

Friday
  Introductions!
Saturday
  Mini-challenge
  Lesson
Sunday
  Lesson
  Mini-challenge
  Lesson
Monday
  Mini-challenge
  Lesson
  Mini-challenge

Tuesday
  Field trip challenge
Wednesday
  Free day—no challenges,
  but a surprise awaits!
Thursday
  Elimination challenge
  with the judges

No one moved. There was a lot to take in. Oliver, Rae, and Caroline studied the paper. Tate counted the days on his fingers. Chef Nancy smiled and waited. When they looked up again, she asked again.

"Are you ready for fun?"

This time they all answered.

"YEAH!"

....

After breakfast, Chef Nancy led the group to the school studio. It was smaller than the filming studio, but the workstations were identical. Instead of a pantry, there was a large curtain at the front of the room.

Tate ran to his workstation. "Can we touch stuff?"

"Great idea." Chef Nancy nodded. "Let's take fifteen minutes to explore your spaces."

Rae opened and closed all the drawers, a huge smile on her face. "I can't believe it. There are so many tools!"

Caroline fiddled with the food processor. "This is the exact same one my mom has in her restaurant."

"Good weight!" said Tate. He handled one of the knives.

"Can we move things around?" asked Oliver. "I like my measuring tools on the left side of my workstation."

"Me too!" said Tate, and he grinned at Oliver.

"Of course," said Chef Nancy. "This is your space. You make the rules."

....

The fifteen minutes passed quickly. Not everyone was happy.

"Already?" complained Tate. "But I didn't even get to look at the mixer!"

Chef Nancy nodded in sympathy, but she didn't change her mind. Instead, she walked to the large curtain at the front of the room and flung it open.

Tate gasped, instantly forgetting his frustration.

Chef Nancy waved her arm. "I present the Gadget Wall!"

She gave everyone a minute to look it over. The entire wall was filled with spinners, slicers, strainers, spatulas, tongs, knives—cooking gadgets of every kind.

Before anyone could ask any questions, Chef Nancy continued. "If you win a mini-challenge, you can choose your prize from this wall. That item will be yours to take home, but until then, please keep all gadget prizes in the toolbox under your workstation. Your gadgets are not to be used in the competition."

Tate nodded. "I wondered what that box was for."

Caroline nodded. "Me too. I looked—it's empty."

"Not for long," bragged Oliver.

TATE

When I win a mini-challenge, I'm going to pick a chef's knife! I like chopping and slicing. I taught myself by watching YouTube videos. My mom calls me Master Chopper, but that's embarrassing, so I don't tell people. Oops! Oh, man—now everyone knows.

CHAPTER 6

Chef Nancy pointed to the door. "Okay, everyone, let's move over to the filming studio. We'll be using the pantry in our first challenge."

Two workers brushed past as they walked out.

"Let them through," said Chef Nancy. "They're here to get the Gadget Wall and bring it to the filming studio."

Tate stopped and looked back. "They're taking down the wall?"

Rae pushed him forward. "It has wheels!"

"How did you know?"

Rae shrugged. "I notice stuff."

Steve was waiting in the filming studio with the camerapeople Janet and Mark.

Chef Nancy stepped next to Steve and raised her hand. "Workstations, please—and don't touch anything."

But it was too late; Tate was already waving a handful of

cards he'd picked up off his table. "What are these for? Are we playing a card game?"

Steve scowled.

Chef Nancy waved her arms. "STOP! You may touch the cards, but PLEASE! Do not touch anything else! Especially the aprons!"

Steve glared at Tate, but only Rae noticed. She turned back to her apron and smiled. There it was, her name, right under the *Next Best Junior Chef* logo. She couldn't wait to put it on.

My *wow* moment was seeing the apron with my name on it. It made everything seem more real. I got goose bumps all over my arms!

RAE

"These are camera cards," said Chef Nancy. She waved one in the air. "You each have ten camera cards, and it's in your best interest to keep them and not lose them. The camera card competition starts today and finishes on Wednesday. The contestant with the most cards left on Wednesday afternoon will be the camera card winner."

"How do you lose them?" asked Caroline.

"Camera mistakes." Chef Nancy shook her head. "I don't like to do it, but if you purposely look directly at the camera, perform for the camera, or hide from the camera, I will have to ask you to give up one of your camera cards."

Rae pointed to the Gadget Wall. "Is the prize a gadget?"

"Better," said Chef Nancy. "The prize is an hour-long private cooking lesson with me on Wednesday night."

"Wait!" Tate waved his cards again. "That's huge! Isn't the elimination challenge on Thursday? And the winner gets a special lesson ahead of everyone else! Is it a lesson on anything we want?"

Chef Nancy waved her arm over the room. "Anything you want."

Tate nodded. Chef Nancy was right: a private lesson was better than a gadget, and probably worth more than a mini-mixer, a fancy cheese grater, and a really good knife all put together.

"I need that!" announced Caroline.

"Me too," added Rae.

"Good luck!" said Oliver, but Rae could tell he didn't mean one bit of it.

Steve nodded to Chef Nancy. "Okay, junior chefs, this is our first mini-challenge. The cameras are about to go on, and they will be following you into the pantry, so watch for them. No pushing, please."

Steve held up his hand and spun it in a circle. "ROLLING!"

That word sent a nervous shiver straight down Caroline's spine. Rae shot her a fast smile. It helped. Caroline nodded back.

OLIVER

I like the cameras. It's important to catch all the big moments in the competition. Plus, a real chef knows how to work under pressure. They don't bother me at all.

Chef Nancy clapped her hands. "Okay, contestants, this is the moment you've been waiting for. Please put on your aprons."

Tate wasn't sure if he was supposed to stay quiet, but he couldn't. "AWESOME!"

Rae felt exactly the same.

Putting on the apron was a big moment. It was exciting but it also made me feel calm. The apron is my uniform. When I'm wearing it, it means I'm doing my favorite thing in the world: cooking!

CAROLINE

••••

The first mini-challenge was a game called Pantry Pick-Up.

Chef Nancy stood at the table at the front of the room and

explained the rules. "This game is designed to help you learn the layout of the pantry. You will each get a list of ten different items to collect and put into your basket. The first one back here with all the correct items will be the winner."

TATE

What did I do to prepare for this mini-challenge? Jumping jacks and squats. A warm body moves faster than a cold body, and to win you have to be fast!

CHAPTER 7

C hef Nancy held her hand up. "Your time starts . . ." She sliced the air. "Now!"

Everyone raced to the pantry. Rae stopped next to the arugula and read over her list.

"Watch it!" Tate sprinted around her.

There were ten items on the list; and two had pictures. That was helpful, because she had no idea what a fiddlehead or a sunchoke even was. She found the sunchokes next to the potatoes. The sunchoke is not an attractive vegetable. It's like the zombie cousin to the potato—nobby, brown, and misshapen. The fiddleheads didn't look much better to Rae. They reminded her of curled-up green caterpillars. It was a relief to get to the familiar. She looked for the easy things next: Parmesan cheese, spaghetti noodles, cilantro, sour cream, and peanut butter. The cumin was easy too—spices were always in alphabetical order. She found the whole-wheat flour next. It was heavy and hard to carry around—that was bad planning. She should have left it for last. She ran her finger over the list—one item left.

"Bosc pear!" Rae shouted out loud, but no one noticed. They were too busy racing around and yelling. Mostly it was *Excuse me! Excuse me! Excuse me!* But then there was something different.

"BEHIND YOU!"

A second later, there was a crash.

Tate and Oliver were on the ground, their baskets empty and food all over the floor. Tate scrambled up, scowling. Oliver shrugged and brushed himself off. Rae went back to the pears. This wasn't as easy as she thought it'd be. She stared at the display. There were four different kinds of pears; red, yellow, green, brown—and no labels. Which one was the Bosc pear?

"Time!" shouted Chef Nancy.

"What, already?" Tate dropped his basket.

Chef Nancy had one hand in the air and the other on Caroline's shoulder. It was only a game, but still, Rae was disappointed. It's not easy to go from *I could win this* to *I lost*.

Chef Nancy called everyone over to the big table. Tate grumbled all the way back. Chef Nancy checked his basket. He was missing a fig and had almond butter instead of almond paste.

Rae was missing a Bosc pear. It was the brown one.

Oliver had everything—but he hadn't made it back to the table before Caroline.

Chef Nancy read from Caroline's list and unloaded her

basket onto the table. "Paprika, asiago cheese, baking soda, buttermilk, tiger melon, celery root, almonds, cornstarch, golden delicious apple, and prunes. Congratulations, Caroline! You have all the items on your list. You are the winner! You may pick your gadget."

Caroline raced over to the Gadget Wall, a camera following closely behind.

Oliver shook his head. "It's too bad I crashed, but I'm happy for Caroline. She must be so excited."

Chef Nancy patted Oliver's shoulder. "Thank you for showing such good sportsmanship. That's an important skill."

"Yes ma'am." Oliver nodded.

"Um." Tate moved next to Oliver. "Sorry about the crash. You could have won."

Oliver smiled. "No worries. It's just a game."

When Caroline came back, Oliver was having his own private interview about being a good team player. They all had to wait until it was over. Rae scowled—even when he lost, Oliver was a winner.

OLIVER

Sure, it was a race, but things can go wrong. If Tate hadn't crashed into me, I probably would have won, but accidents happen. I want everyone to be happy. I don't get upset about little things. I'm the King of Calm in competition and in the kitchen.

When the interview was over, Caroline held up her gadget for everyone to see. It was plastic and tube-shaped. No one knew what it was called or what it was for.

Caroline set it down on the table. "It's a spiral veggie slicer! I saw one once on TV."

Chef Nancy went to the pantry and came back with a zucchini. She handed it to Caroline for a demonstration. Caroline went right to work.

"Zucchetti!" joked Tate, and it was true. The slicer could turn a zucchini into strands that looked just like spaghetti.

Oliver put his hand up. "Can we play again?"

"Of course," said Chef Nancy. "But before we do, does anyone have any thoughts on how to save time?"

"Get the heavy things last."

"Put the list in order of where the items are in the pantry."

"Get what you know first."

"Go to the fridge last—that door is super heavy."

They all agreed about the door.

Chef Nancy shook her head. "I'm sorry about that. We can't change the door."

My dad's in the army, so he knows all about working out. We used to do a routine together every morning. I'm still practicing for when he gets back. Tomorrow I'll add some extra push-ups. That'll help with the fridge door.

TATE

CHAPTER 8

There were three more rounds of Pantry Pick-Up. Oliver won a mandolin and a kitchen torch and Rae won a food scale.

"Why did you pick that?" asked Caroline.

Rae carefully placed the scale into her toolbox, then looked up. "Recipes from other countries use weight as a measurement, not cups and tablespoons. Now I can make anything."

Chef Nancy had to take two camera cards away from Tate. "You can't look directly into the camera and smile."

Tate slumped and shuffled his feet. "I know, but my mom always says *Smile for the camera*. So it's hard not to. She trained me."

Chef Nancy tried to hide her smile. It wasn't the excuse she was expecting. "Okay, but please try to ignore the cameras while we're filming."

Tate nodded, but then frowned.

Rae looked at Caroline and made a sad face. Poor Tate. The mini-challenges were over and everyone had a prize except for him.

····

After lunch, it was "camera time." That's what Chef Nancy called the extra shots Steve the producer wanted. They filmed some close-ups: Rae's hand picking fiddleheads from the pantry, Tate filling up his basket with rainbow carrots, Caroline opening the heavy fridge door, and then the rest was all Oliver . . . and his hand. Oliver's hand was like the superstar of the day! There were close-ups of his hand holding a cantaloupe, choosing arugula, reaching high on the spice shelf for anise, picking up oyster mushrooms off the floor to put back into the overturned basket, and then finally holding a small quail's egg. Oliver acted like it was no big deal, but it was obvious he loved it.

RAE

I'm super excited to show the judges my idea for my food truck if I win. I don't want to give it away, but it has something to do with this charm on my necklace. I make charms all the time. This one's for my grandma. I made a clay teacup, because we have tea together every day at four o'clock. She's the one who started me cooking and crafting. My two favorite things!

....

Oliver, Rae, Tate, and Caroline were in the filming studio, waiting. The judges were late. It was hard to be excited and still at the same time. Tate did some jumping jacks. Chef Nancy rushed over and straightened his hair. She was pickier when the judges were around. Suddenly a door opened and Chef Gary, Chef Aimee, and Chef Porter walked into the room. Instantly, everything got a lot more exciting!

While the judges got themselves seated at the big table, Chef Nancy whispered some last-minute instructions to the junior chefs. "Cameras are on. Remember: Don't look at the cameras. Look at the judges."

The judges were going to call them up separately for a sit-down chat. This was a lot more special than lining up in a row. And they'd all get the exact same question. *If you become the Next Best Junior Chef, what will your food truck be?*

My food truck is called the Crafty Café. It will serve food and will have all sorts of craft kits for sale. People will come to eat good food and do crafts together.

RAE

OLIVER

My food truck is called Bistro Revilo. I'll serve organic and locally sourced food. The menu will be creative bistro food. *Revilo* is Oliver spelled backwards. It's perfect, because I did a twist with my name and I'll add a twist to bistro food, too.

My food truck will be called Diner Française. I love American diners, but mine will serve diner food with a French twist. It'll be a creative mix of flavors. The first thing I want on the menu is croissants filled with cereal-infused pastry cream.

CAROLINE

TATE

My food truck will be called Stuff My Face. I'll serve a mashup of foods; there won't be a set menu. One day it could be Japanese inspired, the next Korean, or Greek. People will come back because they will want to try new things. And if someone asks where they're going for lunch, they can say, "I'm going to Stuff My Face!"

....

The judges really liked the Crafty Café, Bistro Revilo, and Diner Française. When Tate presented Stuff My Face, Chef Gary laughed, Chef Aimee smiled, but not Chef Porter—she only frowned.

"It's clever," said Chef Gary.

"It's funny," said Chef Aimee.

"It's fine," said Chef Porter, but her face looked as if she'd just eaten a super-sour pickle.

Tate withered like spinach in a pan—all his energy instantly gone. He took his place next to Oliver, close to tears.

CHAPTER 9

hef Nancy looked at Tate. The double negative—no wins and a bad review from Chef Porter—had taken its toll. He stood motionless, head down and shoulders drooped. Thankfully there was still time to turn things around. Knife skills were next. She looked at her watch—yes, there was time. She'd add a chopping challenge. Tate was a master chopper, and hopefully this would improve his mood.

Chef Nancy glanced around the filming studio. The contestants were at their workstations, the Gadget Wall was in place, and the medics were seated. Medics were present for all cooking and knife-related lessons and challenges. Safety was important.

She made her announcement. "Next up we'll have a knife skills lesson and then a chopping mini-challenge." She snuck a peek at Tate. He was listening and straightened up, surprised.

Chef Nancy always started the knife lesson with a paper test. A sharp knife was a chef's best friend. A dull knife was dangerous. She had everyone hold up a piece of paper and then slice it in half. That was the test of a truly sharp knife.

Everyone knew the basics: pinch grip for holding the knife, and claw grip for holding whatever you were cutting. Safety and calm were essential when using knives, so timed challenges were out. Chopping challenges were graded solely

on skill. Chef Nancy held up three carrots. She sliced the first one paper-thin, then used the batonnet cut to turn the other two into sticks. She held them up for everyone to see, and then chopped some more until she had an assortment of large, medium, and small cubes.

She picked up one of the tiniest cubes. "Does anyone know the name of this cut?" Tate, Oliver, and Caroline all raised their hands. Chef Nancy pointed to Tate.

"Brunoise cut." He grinned, bouncing up and down. It was his specialty.

Steve and the camerapeople came in just as the lesson was finishing up. Mark and Janet quickly took their places.

A minute later, Steve gave the start signal. "Rolling!"

Chef Nancy held up an onion, a turnip, and a potato. "This challenge is not about time—it's about perfection. I want you to turn this potato into tiny cubes, this onion into paper-thin slices, and this turnip into perfectly julienned strips. You may begin."

Tate peeled his potato, cut it in half, then used the batonnet cut, just as Chef Nancy had demonstrated. Minutes later perfect tiny cubes fell onto his cutting board. When Tate was chopping, his feet didn't bounce and his concentration didn't waver. He was calm and careful. At the end of the challenge, Tate had the largest amount of perfectly sliced onions, julienned turnips, and cubed potatoes.

"Congratulations, Tate! You are the winner. You may

choose an item from the Gadget Wall." Chef Nancy breathed a sigh of relief.

Tate jumped up, high-fived the air, and raced off to the wall. Seconds later he was walking back—carefully—holding a Santoku knife.

"Nice choice." Chef Nancy nodded approvingly.

Tate grinned.

Oliver was surprised by Tate's win. "Tate has knife skills?"

Rae beamed. "I know, isn't that great? Now we all have prizes."

Caroline didn't say anything, because she was crying. The tears were mostly from the onion, but a few were for something else. Chef Nancy was holding one of her camera cards.

"I'm sorry, Caroline. You can't turn your back and try to hide from the cameras. They need to be able to see what you're doing."

Caroline sniffled and nodded. The cameras were always watching, ready to catch any mistake. Just thinking about it made her hand shake. Not a good thing when she was in the middle of chopping up a turnip.

I'm glad Tate won. His food truck idea was kind of a bomb. This might help him feel a little better. It's hard when you disappoint the judges. That's not something you can easily forget.

OLIVER

fter dinner, the junior chefs had time to video-chat with their families.

RAE

> Even though we're away from home, it's not so bad, because I get to talk to my grandma every day. She wants to know everything I'm doing. If there was a *Next Best Grandma Chef*, she'd win for sure. She's a great chef and she likes learning new things.

Tate told his mom about smiling for the camera.

She shook her head. "You're right! It's my fault. Forget I ever said it! Don't listen to me!"

He didn't tell her about Chef Porter and his food truck idea. Moms didn't need to know everything.

Before saying goodbye, his mom leaned forward until the whole screen was just her nose and a giant eye. "And you be careful with those knives! Do you promise?" And then she whispered, "Master Chopper."

"Mom!" Tate put his hand over his heart. "I promise."

····

Rae sat on the side of her bed and went over the day in her head. She felt comfortable in her workstation, she'd learned her way around the pantry, she'd had good interviews, and she'd even won a mini-challenge. That was a lot for one day. And best of all, *everyone* was happy. She'd been worried about Tate, but at the last minute . . .

". . . Tate won!"

Caroline sat up and leaned over. "I know! I'm happy for him too!"

Rae turned, surprised. Was Caroline a mind reader?

Caroline smiled. "You talk to yourself. That's okay—I do too, but not as much as you."

Rae blushed.

Caroline lowered her voice. "Poor Tate. Chef Porter's a little scary."

Rae looked up. "A little?"

Caroline laughed. "Okay, a lot."

Rae shook her head. "She doesn't like kids."

"Except Oliver." Caroline's face got serious. "You can tell by the way she looks at him."

Rae scrunched up her nose. "That's because Oliver is like

a grownup in a kid body. He doesn't act like a kid, or even look like one. He wears shirts like my dad. Don't you think he's a little strange?"

"But he saved you," said Caroline.

"Caught me," corrected Rae. "Saved and caught are different."

"Well, I think he's okay. Maybe not super friendly, but Tate likes him."

"Tate likes everybody."

Caroline laughed. "Not true." And then she made a face like she'd just eaten a sour pickle. It was a good Chef Porter impression.

Rae dissolved into giggles.

....

Tate and Oliver were supposed to be sleeping, but Oliver had a question. Something he needed to know.

"That knife thing today—how come you were so good at it? Did you take lessons?"

Tate shook his head. "Not really. I just watched some YouTube videos and then practiced a lot."

"So no one came over and gave you lessons? Or gave you lessons at a restaurant?"

"No—do people do that? Is that a thing?"

Oliver lay back down. "Maybe."

Tate wasn't giving up. "Do you know someone who did that?"

Oliver grumbled, "I know someone who wants to sleep." Then he turned and pulled the covers right over his head.

CHAPTER 11

C hef Nancy watched everyone file into the filming studio. Caroline and Rae were whispering to each other, Tate was hopping up and down next to Oliver, and the King of Calm seemed cool and collected. This was the way to start a day.

Chef Nancy clapped her hands to get their attention. "Can anyone tell me what plating is?"

"Making food look nice on the plate," answered Tate.

Chef Nancy nodded. "True, but it's more than that. It's an important step in sharing the eating experience. Seeing the food leads to eating the food, which leads to enjoying the food. And as a chef, your job is to make each of these steps as enticing and as pleasurable as possible."

"What about smelling the food?" asked Caroline.

"Of course," said Chef Nancy. "That too."

Chef Nancy handed out big white boards and small plastic containers of sauce—a red one and a green one.

Rae rubbed her hand over the surface of the board, then rested it against her cheek. "It's smooth and cool like a dinner plate."

Chef Nancy nodded. "Good catch. These are porcelain boards. This is the same material used to make fine china . . . which means they're breakable, so don't drop them."

Tate held up the green container. "Can we eat it?"

Caroline frowned. "We just had breakfast!"

"I know. I was only wondering."

Chef Nancy ignored Tate and continued. She held up the red sauce. "We're going to practice our decorating skills. You can do a lot with a thin sauce. Drop a dollop onto the board, clean the back of the spoon, and then drag the spoon through the sauce. Practice some spoon drags. Try making swirls, zigzags, and circles. The green sauce is thicker, more of a purée . . . and definitely NOT for eating!" She looked at Tate. "You'll want to try more of a smear after you get it on the board. If your board fills up, just wipe it off and start again."

Chef Nancy wandered around the room while everyone was practicing.

"This green sauce is impossible!" complained Tate. "It's too blobby."

"Don't press so hard," suggested Caroline. "Try smooth and slow."

"My swirls aren't great either," confessed Rae. "It's good that food goes on top to cover the mistakes."

"Don't give up," said Chef Nancy encouragingly. "It's

better to practice now, when you have the time and no one is judging you."

Oliver practiced his smears and swirls, but he didn't need to—he was an expert already. He'd learned from the best. There were two world-class restaurants in his hometown, and the head chefs had helped him. He'd gone for lessons six Saturdays in a row. It was kind of a surprise that no one else had done that. Or maybe they were like him, keeping it secret. Self-taught sounded a lot more impressive than private lessons. He dropped a dollop of red sauce on his board and made a swirly double *S*.

"Perfect!" Whatever the challenge, he was going to win.

Some people have the desire to practice and some people just have talent. I'm lucky. I have both.

OLIVER

TATE

I know looks are important, but isn't taste more important? I never judge food until after the first bite. That's only fair.

CHAPTER 12

hef Nancy called the junior chefs up to the front table to explain the next mini-challenge.

"Each of you will be given a surprise box. These boxes contain three plates, three proteins, three sauces, three salads, and various garnishes. When we start, you'll have fifteen minutes to assemble three beautifully plated meals. Just so you know, the proteins look real, but they're plastic. We don't want to waste food if we don't have to. And remember, when I call time, I want all your hands in the air. No last-minute changes."

She looked around the room nodding, making sure they each nodded back.

She clapped her hands. "Okay, everyone—places."

A minute later they were starting.

"Rolling!" shouted Steve.

TATE

The first thing I did was take everything out of the box and arrange it on my table. You have to think about color and texture when you're plating. A good dish has a combination of colors, textures, and shapes. Something fun for your eyes and something fun for your mouth.

There were rules for plating and Rae knew them. She put a few of the plastic shrimp to the side. A good chef plated in odd numbers, threes or fives, not fours. Asymmetry, an uneven plate, was always more interesting. Rae picked out a

round plate and dropped three dollops of yellow sauce in the middle. She swirled the sauce out from the center of the plate, then placed the three shrimp in the white space between the swirls. Pale shrimp, a white plate, yellow sauce—she needed some color.

She chose a slaw dotted with bright red pomegranate seeds and arranged a small mound in the center of the plate.

The red seeds added a nice pop of color. Leaving white space on the plate was important, so Rae was careful with the microgreens—not too many, just enough to engage the eye to move around the plate.

She looked it over. "Good enough to eat, except it's plastic."

Oliver was just finishing up his last plate when Chef Nancy called time. He put his hands in the air—triumphant. His plates looked amazing! The edges were clean, the swirls were perfect, and the plastic food looked delicious.

Chef Nancy walked from station to station examining the plates.

Oliver scanned the room. Rae was his only competition. He knew that even though he couldn't see her plates. She was good at decorating stuff, probably because she made all those tiny clay charms. He studied Caroline. What a mess. There was green sauce everywhere—on her face, on her apron, and on the edge of one of her plates—that was definitely not on purpose. She'd lose points for that. He wasn't worried about Tate. Sure, he could chop, but he didn't have the patience for plating. His plates were busy: too many elements, oversize portions, and no focal point for the eye. Oliver leaned forward, trying to see Rae's plates, but Chef Nancy was standing in the way. He clenched and unclenched his hands. He had to win! Winning today would be an advantage for tomorrow. With three wins he'd be in the lead. He deserved that!

I won the plating challenge! I can't believe it. My best plate was definitely the lamb chops. I stacked them crisscross on a bed of wrapped asparagus next to a trio of mini potatoes, onions, and carrots. I framed the whole thing with a swirl of brown and yellow sauce radiating out from the center of the plate. It's not my fault that someone forgot to add his carrots. This is a competition. It could have been me, but it wasn't.

RAE

····

Everyone walked back to the lodge, except Tate—he ran. After lunch there were going to be private interviews in a special room.

Caroline complained and scratched her hand. "Why do we have to be interviewed all alone, by ourselves? What do you think they'll ask us?"

Rae had some ideas. "Maybe it's about special skills or secret recipes."

Oliver stepped between them and grumbled, "It won't be that."

He lowered his voice. "They're going to ask us our true feelings. What we really think of each other."

CHAPTER 13

Caroline was the first person interviewed. She went into the room nervous and jittery but came out smiling. She walked straight to Rae.

"It wasn't so bad. Mostly they wanted to know if I was intimidated by anyone's skills, and who I thought was the most talented person here."

Rae sighed. "Oh, good, so Oliver was wrong. Do you think he said all that on purpose, just to get me worried, because I won and he was mad about his carrots?"

Caroline shrugged. "Don't you want to know who I picked? Caroline's choice for most talented chef?"

"Who?"

"Guess?"

Rae rolled her eyes. She wasn't in a mood for jokes.

"Okay fine, I picked . . . ME!"

"You?" For a second Rae was surprised, but she shouldn't

have been. That's why they were here—to win, no matter what. And to win, friends had to beat friends.

CAROLINE

Everyone's so nice. I like Rae and Tate, and Oliver—well, he's special, because he's sort of a hero and he's a really good cook, too. It's hard to tell who'll be the best, but I think I have a really good chance. I won't give up. I want to win. That's my dream.

····

Rae's turn was next, and Chef Nancy walked with her to the bright orange door. There were two stools in the room, and two cameras pointed toward the empty one. Steve was sitting on the other one. He motioned for Rae to sit down. Mark and Janet did not wave.

"Are you okay?" Chef Nancy tapped Rae's shoulder. "Comfortable? Need anything?"

Rae shook her head.

"Great. Have fun. I'll see you in a few minutes."

As soon as Chef Nancy closed the door, the interview started.

"So, Rae, tell us: what inspires you and your cooking?"

"What inspires me and my cooking are the people in my

neighborhood. They're from all over the world, and they like to share their recipes. Mrs. Demir lives two trailers away and she showed my grandma and me how to make baklava, but she makes something even more unbelievable. It's called tavukgogs—it's a dessert pudding made with chicken. I haven't tried that yet." Rae scowled. "I'm not sure I would like it."

Steve nodded. "Well, you seem a lot more confident than when we first met you. Do you remember that first day? Can you believe that was only two days ago?"

Rae scowled again. She didn't like thinking about the fainting.

Steve's face got serious. "Who do *you* think should win the title of Next Best Junior Chef?"

Rae smiled—easy answer. "Me! I've worked hard to get here and I won't stop working. I should win the title of Next Best Junior Chef."

Steve took some notes and then looked up. Serious face again. "And the other contestants . . . what do you think of Oliver? He saved you. Any special feelings?"

Rae's eyes widened, then narrowed. She shook her head.

"Oliver didn't save me! He caught me. There's a difference. It was nice of him, but it doesn't mean we have to be friends or anything. Oliver spends most of his time thinking about Oliver. I don't think he cares about friends."

Steve grinned and nodded.

"Great interview, Rae. Thank you!"

Rae was not like Caroline. She did not leave the interview room smiling.

Oliver was curious. When she walked by, he threw out a "So, how did it go?"

Rae ignored him and kept walking. Oliver watched Rae and Caroline huddling and whispering. He shrugged. Probably girl stuff, but then a moment later, they were staring straight back at him.

CHAPTER 14

liver wasn't worried about the interview. In fact, he couldn't wait for it to happen. He'd heard what Chef Nancy had said about acting up for the cameras, but he was keeping his options open. If the truth needed to be twisted, he could twist it. He had come here with two missions: to win and to look good on TV. And no matter what, he was going to succeed.

When it was his turn, he waved off Chef Nancy.

"Thank you, ma'am, but I'm fine alone." He didn't need an escort. He knew where he was going and what he was going to say. He had it all worked out. He'd start with a positive and end with a negative. Rae was determined but nervous. Caroline was considerate but careless. Tate was energetic but impulsive. And then he'd talk about himself. He was the King of Calm. He thought things through. He saw the big picture. He was serious. He wasn't worried about the others. His path was a straight line to the big prizes.

He sat on the stool, looked directly at Steve, and smiled.

Chef Nancy popped in for a last-minute check. "Everything okay? Comfortable?"

Oliver nodded. He was going to be good at this.

"Rolling." Steve motioned to the cameras and then grinned.

"So, Oliver, can you tell us why everyone except Rae thinks you're a hero?"

For the first time in maybe his entire life, Oliver couldn't think of a single thing to say.

Well, Rae and I don't even really know each other, so how can she say those things? Of course I care about friends. I care about people. I saved her, didn't I? Some people just don't know how to say thank you.

OLIVER

As soon as Tate was done with his interview, Chef Nancy hurried everyone over to the school studio for a lesson. The looks between Oliver and Rae split the group in two. Oliver and Tate walked ahead, Caroline and Rae behind, and no one said anything.

TATE

Oliver is a hero. We all think so. What he did for Rae was amazing. I can't wait to see if he's a hero in the kitchen, too. I guess that would be bad for me, but I'm not scared of a little competition. I'm little, but I have lots of energy.

CHAPTER 15

Everyone filed quietly into the room, but Chef Nancy didn't notice the mood. The lesson on taste and the tongue was one of her favorites, and she couldn't wait to get started.

"Who knows where the taste buds are?"

"On your tongue," answered Oliver.

Chef Nancy nodded. "And how many do you think there are?"

Tate made a guess. "Two hundred?"

"More," said Chef Nancy. "Somewhere between two thousand and five thousand. And there are taste buds under your tongue, on the roof and sides of your mouth, and in your throat. These taste buds tell us what we're tasting. Can anyone name the primary tastes and give a food example?"

"Sweet like sugar and sour like vinegar," said Oliver. He shot a look at Rae.

She whispered something to Caroline.

Then Rae sneered and put up her hand. "Salty like soy sauce, and bitter like coffee. Coffee smells good, but the taste of it can make you gag. Some things only seem good on the outside."

"Excellent," said Chef Nancy. "There's one more."

"Chocolate!" said Tate.

That wasn't the right answer, but it made Chef Nancy smile. She loved chocolate. "This fifth taste is a tricky one. A Japanese researcher discovered it in 1910. It's called *umami,* and is described as the ability to taste savory or meaty deliciousness. Parmesan cheese, steak, sardines, ripe tomatoes, black olives, and mushrooms all have umami. It's the yummy taste."

Chef Nancy smiled at the group, but only Tate and Caroline smiled back. "Knowing the science behind taste can make you a better chef. It can also help you describe your dishes."

Tate waved his hand. "What if you don't like sardines—then it's not yummy, is it?"

Chef Nancy nodded. "True, not everyone likes the same things, but even if you don't like something, your taste buds are still tasting it. Do you like sardines?"

Tate shook his head.

Rae scrunched up her nose. "And I don't like olives because—"

"I do!" interrupted Oliver. "Olives are sophisticated." He

crossed his arms and sneered. He kept quiet about not liking mushrooms. No one needed to know he wasn't perfect.

Chef Nancy studied Rae, then Oliver. Was something going on?

Rae leaned close to Caroline and whispered. "*Oliver* and *olives* are almost spelled the same. Do you think that's why I don't like them?" Rae leaned back, waiting for Caroline to agree.

Caroline shuffled uncomfortably. She liked both Rae and Oliver. What was she supposed to say? Instead of an answer, she blurted out her secret. The thing she wasn't going to tell anyone. "Cilantro tastes like soap."

"What?" Rae was surprised. "No it doesn't!"

Chef Nancy raised her hand. "Wait, it's true! Some people are born with a gene that makes cilantro taste like soap." She nodded to Caroline. "It's genetic—they can't help it."

Rae leaned over to Caroline. "I'm sorry you can't like cilantro."

Caroline shrugged. "What if it does taste like soap and *you're* the one who can't tell?"

Rae made a face. She hadn't thought about it that way.

The rest of the lesson continued without incident. Rae and Oliver were mostly quiet.

Chef Nancy noticed, but she didn't say anything. "The way you describe your food is important, especially in this competition. You will want to choose words that compliment the delicious meals you make. Who can think of a fancy way to say 'mashed'?"

"Puréed!" shouted Tate.

"Whipped," offered Caroline.

"Exactly!" Chef Nancy clapped her hands together. "Words can be powerful. The right language can change the way someone thinks about your food. It might even convince them it tastes better. Which sounds better: scrambled eggs with tomatoes and onions or whipped eggs with a tomato onion relish? Remember, when you're describing your food to the judges, make an effort to be creative. It could make a difference."

CHAPTER 16

Every morning before breakfast, Chef Nancy had a meeting with Steve. It was routine—they went over the schedule, made small changes, and talked about what was coming up. Today he was more excited than usual. He couldn't stop talking about Oliver and Rae. Would they become rivals? Would they feud in front of the cameras? Would the other kids take sides?

Steve rubbed his hands together. "Those interviews yesterday were fantastic! The tension between those two is great for TV. Audiences love drama. This could really boost our ratings."

Chef Nancy smiled like she was agreeing, but she wasn't. She didn't want the kids to have drama; she wanted them to have fun. While she listened to Steve, her brain got working on a new idea. Was there a way to change a rival into a friend?

At the end of the meeting, Steve had one more change.

"Let's add some interviews after breakfast. I don't want to miss an opportunity. They might say something intriguing."

Chef Nancy nodded and gave him a thumbs-up. There was no arguing with Steve. He was the boss.

....

"More interviews?" Caroline crossed her arms. "Why do we have to do so much talking?"

Chef Nancy sighed. What she really wanted to say was *I'm sorry you have to do more interviews. The producer is sneaky!*

But she couldn't say that, so instead she tried to be positive: "It'll be fast! The producer is giving you a chance to really shine—to show off your enthusiasm for the show and cooking. Right after the interviews we'll head to the filming studio for a mini-challenge."

Caroline slumped. Chef Nancy's pep talk didn't help. She was tired of the cameras.

I'm going to beat Rae because I'm a better chef. I've had more training than she's had. When you learn from the best, you're going to be the best. Sure, I've had lessons, but that's how you get better. I will win!

OLIVER

Rae came out of her interview smiling, victorious. Steve had tried to trick her, but she was watching for it. Kids could be clever too.

When he asked, *So why do you think you will beat Oliver?* she didn't repeat his question like she was supposed to. Instead, she completely left out Oliver's name.

I'm going to win because I'm smart, I have skills, and I can adapt. I like to try new things.

RAE

Steve grumbled and asked another Oliver question and another, but she did the same thing each time. At the end of the interview, Steve was not smiling.

After a quick beverage break, Chef Nancy marched everyone over to the filming studio. The cameras were waiting and rolling. "Okay, it's time to team up for our next mini-challenge."

"TEAMS?" Tate hopped up and down, looking at Oliver and then Chef Nancy again. "Can we pick our own teams?"

Chef Nancy called Rae to the front. "Rae gets first pick of her teammate, because she won the last challenge."

Rae smiled at Caroline. This was an easy choice.

Chef Nancy held up a green bag. "Time to pick your

partner! There are three envelopes in here, each with a name in it."

Rae's smile disappeared. Chef Nancy held the bag while Rae put her hand in and felt each envelope. Which one was Caroline's, or even Tate's? She closed her eyes and made a wish: *Any name except Oliver's.* But the wish didn't matter, because each envelope was exactly the same, inside and out. It was Chef Nancy's secret; they all said OLIVER.

Rae pulled an envelope halfway out, then changed her mind and chose a different one.

Chef Nancy opened the envelope and read out the winning name.

"Congratulations, Oliver! Come join your partner."

CHAPTER 17

"**R**olling!" shouted Steve.

Everyone gathered around while Chef Nancy explained the mini-challenge. Rae and Oliver stood next to each other, grumpy and uncomfortable.

Chef Nancy smiled. "Here's a clue. The team with the strongest muscles will win this one. Any ideas?"

"Cooking, food, muscles . . ." Rae was thinking out loud.

Caroline's face lit up. "Mussels, the kind from the ocean!"

"Close!" Chef Nancy put a small pot on the table, grabbed a fork, and speared a . . . "Scallop!" She held it up for everyone to see. "This is one of the most famous bivalves of the sea. Did you know that the part we eat is actually the muscle? Fascinating . . . and delicious!" She dropped the scallop back into the pot. "You'll have thirty minutes to create a scallop entrée with an accompanying sauce. The pantry will be open for the entire length of the challenge, so don't worry if you forget something. You can go back."

Chef Nancy handed each team a small glass bowl and sent them back to their workstations. "Oliver and Rae will work at Rae's workstation and Caroline and Tate will work at Tate's workstation."

Caroline nudged Tate and held out the bowl. "Look, only three scallops per team. No room for mistakes."

As soon as everyone was ready, Chef Nancy gave the signal to start. "Let's get cooking!"

Oliver quickly tossed salt and pepper onto the scallops. "Have you cooked these before?"

Rae shook her head.

He reached for a frying pan. "Don't worry—I got this."

Rae scowled. This was going to be a disaster. They were only just starting and already Oliver was bossy.

Chef Nancy waved her arms. "And one more thing . . ."

The room fell silent. "You must work together and divide up the work evenly. I'll be watching you."

Oliver stopped, put down the pan, and turned to Rae. If he wanted to win, he had to let her help. He forced a smile. "We should work together. Do you have any ideas for the sauce?"

Rae was surprised, but not too surprised to contribute. This was her chance. "How about a lemon butter créma?"

Oliver thought for a second, then nodded. "Simple and tangy, but what about adding some basil? It'll give it a little more flavor, but not so much that it overpowers the scallops."

Rae agreed. She'd tried scallops before and they were pretty mild.

Chef Nancy checked in while Rae was zesting a lemon. "Any special strategies?"

Oliver picked up a cutting board. "Scallops cook fast, so we're leaving that until the end. Right now we're both working on the sauce. I'm helping with the prep."

"Like chopping these." Rae tossed three shallots across the counter.

Oliver caught them with one hand.

Chef Nancy nodded. "Good teamwork—keep cooking!" Three steps later, she breathed a sigh of relief. Her plan was working.

Watching the carrots didn't make them roast any faster, but Tate couldn't help it. He checked the oven every thirty seconds. They were critical to the recipe.

TATE

When you have a time limit, you have to think creatively. I used the brunoise cut to make our carrots smaller so they would roast quicker. Roasted carrots have a sweet caramelized taste. It's worth the extra effort, even though they'll end up in a purée.

Chef Nancy peeked over his shoulder. "What's cooking?"

Tate didn't look up. "Not these super slow-roasting carrots!"

"They're for our carrot purée," added Caroline, "to go with savory scallops."

"Sounds delicious. How are you making the purée?"

"Food processor!" they both shouted at once.

Chef Nancy looked at her watch. "Ten minutes left."

Tate pulled the carrots from the oven and checked them. "They're still NOT DONE! We need more roasting time."

Caroline grabbed a spoon and scooped them into the food processor. "There's no more time—we just have to use them as is."

"But . . ." Tate started to protest.

Caroline stopped and turned. "It's better than no sauce."

••••

Time wound down quickly.

"Hot pan, foamy butter—one minute a side. That's how to sear a scallop." Oliver was giving Rae a quick lesson, but something had changed. Instead of sounding bossy, it was helpful.

Caroline dropped a teaspoon of coconut oil into her hot pan, swirled the pan to coat it, and then placed three seasoned scallops in the center.

"Five minutes left!" shouted Chef Nancy.

"TATE! Faster! We have to get that purée done."

Tate held up a jar of honey and shook it. "I CAN'T GET IT OPEN!"

Caroline left the stove to help. She was only gone for a minute, but scallops cook fast. When she got back, two of the scallops were cooked to perfection but the third one was smoking. She scraped it loose from the pan, but it was too late. The underside was charred black. "NO! NO! NO!" Caroline banged her spatula against the stove.

Tate looked worried. "Is there another one?"

Caroline shot him a look.

Tate looked around, then whispered, "We'll cut off the bad part."

Scallops are really hard to cook. You can't forget about them, not even for a second, because they can easily overcook. No one wants to eat a rubbery scallop.

CAROLINE

Janet brought her camera in for a close-up just as Tate was slicing the charred crust off the scallop.

"Great!" grumbled Caroline. "Mistake number one for the whole world to see."

"Wait." Tate shot her a sneaky smile. "If I do this . . ." He turned the cut scallop upside down and placed it on the plate next to the other two. "No one can tell. It looks perfect."

Caroline poked it with her finger. "Rubbery." Hopefully Chef Nancy would try one of the others.

"Thirty seconds," called Chef Nancy. The last seconds of the challenge were loud and busy.

"TIME!" Eight hands shot into the air.

CHAPTER 18

hef Nancy pointed to the front of the room. "Please follow me and bring your dishes to the front table."

Caroline nudged Tate. "You carry it! I'm too nervous."

Tate put the plate down without disturbing even a single microgreen. Caroline studied the competition. Visually they were evenly matched—the real test would be the taste. She rotated the plate so the good scallops were facing out. As long as Chef Nancy didn't choose the bad scallop, they had a chance. Actually more than a chance: Their carrot purée was amazing. It was sweet, rich, and delicious.

Chef Nancy clapped her hands. "I have a surprise! There are three scallops on your plate and only one of me, so let's bring out two more judges!"

Chef Gary Lee and Chef Aimee Copley burst through the doors. Everyone gasped, then clapped and cheered.

Mark zoomed in for close-ups. Rae and Oliver were smiling, but Tate and Caroline looked worried.

"We'll start with Caroline and Tate," said Chef Nancy. Chef Aimee picked up her fork. "Is that carrot mash?"

Tate nodded, then remembered Chef Nancy's lesson about words. "It's a caramelized roasted carrot purée."

Chef Gary grabbed his fork and stabbed a scallop. "Sounds good. My mouth's watering!" He scooped up some of the purée, then delicately took a bite. "Wow . . . Good crunch on the crust. Is that coconut oil?"

Caroline perked up. "Yes, Chef."

"I like the sweetness; it's unexpected."

"Thank you, Chef."

"The purée has a nice flavor, though it might be a little too sweet. The scallops could use just a little more bite. I taste a bit of spice, but with this purée, you could push it more."

Chef Aimee held up her empty fork. "The sweetness works for me . . . plus that scallop was cooked to perfection."

"My turn." Chef Nancy reached in with her fork and speared the last scallop. She took a bite . . .

"AHHHH!!" She spit into her napkin.

"Too sweet?" asked Chef Gary.

"Too rubbery!" Chef Nancy looked at the half scallop still on her fork. "Wait! Why is the end cut off? What happened here?"

There was no choice. Caroline and Tate had to explain.

Chef Gary listened, then shook his head. "That's too bad. Remember, the plate is your stage. If you're not proud of what you've made, leave it off."

"Thank you, Chef." Caroline spoke for the both of them. Tate was too sad to talk.

The judges moved over to Oliver and Rae.

Their expressions said as much as their words. They loved their dish.

"Mmm!" Chef Gary ate his scallop in two fast bites. "The acidity of the basil lemon créma and the perfectly cooked scallop . . . the texture . . . I think I can say . . . I . . . I'm officially speechless! How did you manage such a perfectly seasoned dish? I can't—"

Chef Aimee nudged Chef Gary. "Not so speechless after all."

Everyone laughed.

Chef Gary, Chef Aimee, and Chef Nancy stepped away to discuss the competition, but there was no suspense. It was clear who'd won. When they came back, Chef Gary made the announcement.

"Congratulations, Oliver and Rae. You are the winners of this challenge!"

Rae would have high-fived with Oliver, but he wasn't a high-five kind of guy, so instead they just awkwardly nodded at each other, grinned, and walked over to the Gadget Wall.

"Veggie chopper." Rae held up her pick.

"Micro planer," said Oliver, and he tapped the edge of her chopper.

It was almost like a high-five. Rae smiled.

••••

At lunchtime Caroline piled her plate high with an assortment of potato chips: salt and vinegar, sour cream and onion, salt and pepper, and barbecue.

Oliver was watching. Winning changed his demeanor—it made him friendly and talkative. "How can you eat so much junk food?"

She shrugged. "My mom won't let me have any junk food at home. Plus the one time she did, this happened." She pointed to a scar on the inside of her arm. "Rice Krispie treat burn. I was seven."

"That's nothing!" Tate held out his finger. "Five stitches, and look." He pulled up his pant leg. "Mole sauce burn."

"Mine's new!" Rae held out her wrist. "Baklava. I misjudged how hot the pan was."

Everyone looked at Oliver. He shrugged. "What?"

Rae scowled. All chefs had something. "No fair—we told you ours."

"Fine," grumbled Oliver, "but no laughing." He pushed the hair off his forehead. There was a small circular scar high above his left eye. "I got too close to the toaster when I was six."

Nobody laughed.

Tate leaned in for a better look. "What were you making?"

Oliver shook his head. This was the embarrassing part. "Hot dogs."

"In a toaster?"

"Yup, one popped right out and got me in the head."

They couldn't help it—they had to laugh.

CHAPTER 19

fter lunch there was a lesson and a mini-challenge. No one complained about learning how to make ice cream—this was something they all wanted to try.

Oliver half skipped all the way to the filming studio. Ice cream was one of his all-time favorite foods. In fact, it was number four on the list of what he'd take if he were trapped on a desert island, or, better yet, *dessert* island. He smiled at his silly joke.

Chef Nancy gathered the group for a quick demonstration on making a simple ice cream base.

"Heat the milk and cream, but be careful: don't boil it. While you're waiting, whisk the eggs, sugar, and sweetener. Then, slowly add the hot milk and cream to your egg mixture, a little at a time. Mix and cool. At this point you can add your flavorings. Once everything is cooled, you can put it into the ice cream machine. Save your mix-in ingredients,

like fruit or candy, and add them to your ice cream after it is made. Understand?"

They all nodded enthusiastically. They couldn't wait to get started.

Chef Nancy handed out the camera cards: Tate had eight, Caroline had nine, and Rae and Oliver still had ten.

Oliver glanced at Rae. He wasn't going to lose any camera cards—he was sure of that. All he needed was for Rae to make one mistake. He didn't feel bad. She was probably wishing the same thing about him. A private lesson could be game-changing.

Steve stepped to the front of the room and waved his hand. "Rolling!"

Chef Nancy held up an empty ice cream cone. "Ice cream! It's loved by millions. I want to see innovation. Be inventors! You have ninety minutes to create a unique ice cream flavor. Don't hold back. I want each lick—the first to the last at the very bottom of the cone—to be amazing!" Then she gave the signal. "Let's get cooking!"

They all ran for the pantry with recipes in their heads. Curry mint, bacon fig, strawberry Froot Loops—no two were alike.

"Apple custard pie!" shouted Rae, and she headed straight for the fruit. "Like pasteis de nata, but with apples and cinnamon." Mrs. Souxa, her Portuguese neighbor, made delicious custard tarts. She was the inspiration, and Rae was adding the innovation. She put three apples in her basket. It wasn't like the pears—she knew exactly which ones to pick.

"Honeycrisps." Her favorites for cooking.

The ninety minutes went by fast.

Oliver browned bacon with maple syrup until it was candied and crisp.

Tate simmered milk with coriander, paprika, turmeric, and mint leaves.

Rae caramelized apples in butter and sugar, added extra egg yolks to the recipe for the custard, and whipped up a piecrust.

Caroline soaked sugared cereal in the cream to infuse it with flavor, and then started part two of her recipe—fresh strawberry compote. She dumped the strawberries onto her cutting board and grabbed for a knife, but accidentally nudged her board. The strawberries started to roll.

"NO!" She scrambled to catch them but only saved five—the rest tumbled onto the floor. Caroline bent down to pick them up. When she looked up a camera was staring straight in her face. There were two choices: cry or be brave. She looked up at the camera, blew off a strawberry, and popped it straight into her mouth.

A minute later Chef Nancy was standing in front of her. Caroline handed over her camera card. Obviously she had forgotten the third choice—ignore the camera.

Oliver couldn't wait to use the ice cream maker. This was a professional machine—and that would make a difference. The ice cream would be fantastic. He cooled his base in the freezer to speed up the process.

When it was ready, Mark followed him over to the ice cream maker to catch the action. Oliver held up his mix, smiled at the camera, then emptied the fig cream into the top of the machine. He closed the lid, pushed the button, and waited for the magic to happen.

Minutes later creamy fig ice cream oozed out from the spout. Oliver took it back to his workstation and quickly folded in the candied bacon and ribbons of caramel sauce. He looked up and saw everyone was finished plating—except for him. He rushed to add the finishing touches to his dish just as Chef Nancy called, "Time!"

I made apple custard pie ice cream, with real pastry bites. Custard is creamier than regular ice cream.

RAE

OLIVER

I made fig ice cream with candied bacon and ribbons of chipotle caramel.

I made cereal-infused ice cream with fresh berry compote. I had just enough berries for three scoops of ice cream.

CAROLINE

TATE

I made curry mint ice cream with spiced pistachio crumbles.

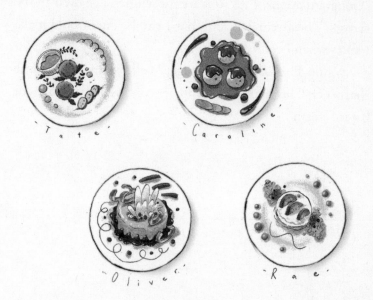

"Amazing! Astounding! Delicious! Addictive!" Chef Nancy loved all of them.

"And cut!" yelled Steve.

Chef Nancy walked toward Oliver. He smiled and eyed the Gadget Wall, but instead of telling him to pick a prize, she asked for one of his camera cards. "Really, Oliver! At this stage, you decide to show off for the camera?" She turned and walked away shaking her head.

Oliver was shocked. He slammed a spoon on the table and his face turned bright red.

Chef Nancy moved to the front of the room and the cameras started again. She called Tate to join her.

"Congratulations, Tate. You are the winner. I enjoyed all the flavors. They were delicious, but I think yours would make me cry when I got to the last lick."

While Tate was at the Gadget Wall picking out a knife sharpener, Chef Nancy filled up her cone with two scoops of his ice cream.

CHAPTER 20

aroline made an extra effort to be nice to Oliver at dinner. He still looked upset, and maybe embarrassed.

Rae was watching him too, but she had different ideas. This was the intimidating boy she'd met on day one. He was angry.

Oliver was trying to calm down, but it wasn't easy. His head felt like a pressure cooker about to explode. Pressure cookers have a little valve on them that slowly lets out the steam. He needed a little valve to let out the steam too.

"Catch." Tate tossed him an orange.

Oliver caught it. He wasn't mad at Tate for winning. Disappointed, sure, but losing the camera card—that's what made him mad. Now Rae would get the private lesson. That was huge. It could change everything, and he'd wasted it for two seconds of happiness on camera.

Oliver tossed the orange back to Tate. They did that for a while, back and forth, neither of them talking.

Then Oliver broke the silence. "Hey, I'm going to check out the library after dinner. Want to come?"

Tate nodded. "Sure." He remembered the library ladders and smiled. After he was done climbing, he'd look up a recipe. His dad had mentioned Gochujang chili paste the last time they'd video-chatted. It was super popular in Korea. He'd seen some in the pantry—maybe he could use it in one of the challenges. His dad would like that. They usually video-chatted twice a week, but now that he was on the show, it was harder—their schedules were different.

••••

Chef Nancy was worried about the next challenge. Oliver was like a pot of noodles about to boil over. What would happen if he lost again? She'd had a talk with him, but she couldn't tell if it had helped. Oliver hadn't said a word, he had only nodded and stared at the floor. This wasn't what she'd been expecting. It was the opposite of calm.

When Oliver and Tate went to the library, Rae and Caroline stayed behind in the lodge. Rae was making a new charm for tomorrow's challenge, and Caroline wanted to help. Rae unpacked her craft bag, laying everything out on the big table in the main room.

"Wow, you have so many colors." Caroline poked at a yellow block of clay. "What kind of clay is this?"

"Plastic. It gets hard in the oven. You can use it too, if you want to make something. Chef Nancy said she'd bake it for us when we're done."

Rae took the teacup charm off her necklace. "Time for something new."

Caroline picked up a small piece of red clay and rolled it between her fingers. "What kind of charm are you making?"

Rae smiled but stayed silent. Caroline would guess soon enough. She formed the clay into a mini apron and centered a red heart on the front. It was an exact replica of the aprons they wore in the competition. She was making two of them, one for each of them, because no matter what happened on Thursday, there was one thing almost as important as winning—to stay friends with Caroline.

CHAPTER 21

Chef Nancy shook her head and pointed to the door. Tate grumbled, turned around, and trudged out of the room. This was strike two. She'd already sent him back once to change his wrinkly shirt, and now he was going again, this time to comb his hair. The field trip challenges were important—the judges would be there, everything had to be perfect, or at least as close as she could get. Oliver walked into the room. Chef Nancy smiled. He didn't need any fashion help. Oliver always wore a pressed button-down shirt.

While everyone ate breakfast, Chef Nancy gave them a rundown of the schedule for the day.

"Chefs, this is a big day: our first field trip challenge! First off, there'll be interviews in the interview room. They'll be brief, so no worries. And then when everyone's done, we'll make our way to the van and depart for the secret destination."

The word *secret* made everyone instantly start talking.

Chef Nancy had to wait, and then wave, to get their attention again.

"Chef Gary and Chef Aimee will meet us at the destination and explain your challenge." Chef Nancy handed everyone a piece of paper. "This is a list of the ingredients that will be available to you at the . . . destination. After breakfast you will have an opportunity to go to the pantry and select three items you would like to bring with you that are not on this list. Please do not pick a main protein. If needed, those will be provided for you."

There were lots of questions.

"Can we bring blue cheese?"

Chef Nancy nodded.

"Dates?"

She nodded again.

"Puff pastry?"

She nodded again. And then after five more times of nodding, once each for wonton skins, pickles, truffle salt, candied ginger, and ancho chili peppers, she pointed to a large cooler on wheels.

"All your special items will go into this cooler. If they can't come, I will let you know."

····

As always, the pantry was well-stocked. There was a wide assortment of fruits, vegetables, and spices, as well as basic cooking supplies like oils, dairy items, and staples. It had everything a chef could want. Rae stopped and looked

around. Usually she had to rush, but today she could take her time. There was even time to talk.

"Where do you think we're going?" asked Tate.

"What do you think we'll be making?" asked Caroline.

Oliver was in a better mood. He joined in too. "Maybe it's a barbecue. It has to be something unusual. Otherwise they'd just have us cooking in the filming studio."

Rae nodded. She hadn't thought about that. Oliver was smart that way. He really thought things through. Oliver picked walnuts, maple syrup, and blue cheese and put them in his basket.

Caroline shook her head. "I hope you're wrong! I've never cooked outside before." She liked a real stove and real tools—the kind you plugged into the wall.

Rae didn't know what to think. Chef Gary had a reputation. He was famous for cooking and eating all sorts of strange things.

"I'll be okay as long as we don't have to cook anything disgusting." Saying it out loud was a mistake—Tate was listening.

He stepped up. "Like what? Fish heads, eyeballs, worms, brains . . . ?"

Rae waved her hands, but did that make him stop? Of course not.

"Tripe, liver . . ."

Rae pushed past him, to get away and to collect her three items. Choosing wasn't easy. She was the last to leave the pantry. She added candied ginger, puff pastry, and ancho chili powder to the cooler. Sweet or savory, she was ready.

I'm hoping the challenge will be a main course with a regular protein, nothing weird. I don't want to say anything bad, but Chef Gary eats stuff I would not want to cook. On one of his shows, he ate stinkbugs.

RAE

OLIVER

I'm hoping the challenge will be upscale barbecue. I like to barbecue in the summer, so I'd be really comfortable with this kind of challenge.

I'm hoping the challenge will be a fancy appetizer or dessert. Maybe we'll get to cook for some famous guests.

CAROLINE

TATE

I'm hoping the challenge will not be a dessert. I checked out some recipes last night and brought some Korean chili paste with me. I really want to try it out and it's too spicy to put in a sweet thing.

CHAPTER 22

he secret destination was forty minutes away. Everyone piled into the van, and on the way, the kids looked out the window for clues.

Apple orchard, blueberry farm, diner, they named off the things they saw.

"Fairground." Caroline pointed. "Look, there's a sign."

Tate read it out loud: "Hendrick's County Fair, three miles." And then a second later he was shouting, "Chef Nancy! Chef Nancy! Is that it? Are we going to the fair?"

Chef Nancy looked back from the passenger seat and shrugged, but everyone noticed that she was smiling.

The next three miles seemed to take forever. Everyone was anxious to get there, especially Caroline. She loved county fairs—she'd been once before, with her summer camp. She'd asked to go again, but her mom wouldn't take her. *Too crowded,* said her mom, *and the smell of frying food makes me nauseous. They use cheap oil and they don't clean their fryers.* Caroline had begged to go, but her mother hadn't changed her mind.

The van let them off at the entrance. Chef Nancy gestured toward the back of the fairground. "We'll have to walk through the whole thing to get to the cooking tent."

Caroline didn't mind—that meant they could look around, but she was wrong. There wasn't time for sightseeing. Chef Nancy was on a mission and moving fast. Caroline had to take running steps just to keep up. Still, no one could stop her from breathing—sweet, salty, oily, spicy . . . Her mother was wrong. The fair smelled delicious.

....

Stepping into the tent was like stepping into the filming studio back at Porter Farm. The workstations were exactly the same. This wasn't an ordinary tent—it had walls on two sides, workstations, an area for the pantry, a sitting area with tables and chairs, and something else behind a big curtain at the very back. Chef Gary Lee and Chef Aimee Copley walked over, a cameraperson following them.

"Welcome! Welcome!" Chef Gary opened his arms. "Are you excited?"

Everyone nodded.

He frowned and cupped his ear. "What? I didn't hear anything."

"YES, CHEF!"

He smiled. "That's more like it. So, what are you going to do today? Any ideas?"

"Ride the roller coaster!"

"Pet the sheep!"

"Eat cotton candy!"

"Cook!" said Oliver.

Chef Gary winked at Oliver. "This young man knows what we're here for. Okay, Chef Aimee, show them what you've got."

Chef Aimee held out two corndogs. "It's food on a stick! And just one of the many different foods on a stick you can find here at the fair. For this challenge we want you to create an upscale savory snack on a stick."

While she talked, she waved them around—like a

conductor with batons. When it got close to Chef Gary, he leaned over and chomped.

"AAAH!" Chef Aimee screamed and the corndogs went flying.

Tate laughed so hard he snorted.

Chef Gary held up his hand, chewed, and then swallowed. "Delicious! But it might have been better with . . . Any ideas from our young chefs?"

"Mustard aioli," said Oliver.

"Red pepper sauce," said Tate.

"Melted brie," said Caroline.

"Cilantro pesto," said Rae.

Chef Gary licked his lips and leaned toward Chef Aimee.

"I think we've picked the right young chefs for this competition."

He turned back to the kids.

"We can't wait to see what you come up with. For inspiration, we're going to send you out into the fair in pairs, to see how many snacks on a stick you can find. We'll meet back here in an hour."

The cameras turned off and Chef Gary came over and shook everyone's hand.

Chef Aimee patted Caroline on the shoulder. "Remember, have fun."

Caroline nodded. That wouldn't be hard. The fun part had already started.

aroline grabbed Rae's hand and swung it high in the air. "I'm so glad we got to pick our own partners!"

"Me too!" Rae gave her a fast hug.

Before they went off to explore the fair, Chef Nancy explained the rules. "You'll have money and be on your own except for the camerapeople. Tate and Oliver, you'll have Janet, and Rae and Caroline, you'll have Mark. They'll be following you and filming everything."

Chef Nancy handed each group a basket and then pointed to her watch. "Janet and Mark will keep track of the time, and signal you when you need to head back."

Mark and Janet gave Chef Nancy a thumbs-up.

Chef Nancy was still talking, but Caroline heard only bits and pieces. "Not a race . . . come back with samples . . . cover different areas." It was hard to concentrate on the words, because her nose was working overtime. What was that delicious smell? Kettle corn? Corn fritter? Donut?

And then Rae was pulling her hand. She'd missed the signal. The hour was starting.

••••

Food on a stick was not hard to find. The hard part was not eating it.

Caroline held a deep-fried Oreo up to her nose and sniffed.

Rae poked her. "No licking!"

Caroline nodded and put the Oreo down, but Rae didn't trust her. She took the basket away.

"I'll carry it."

"Good thinking." Caroline licked her fingers. "I don't trust me either."

At first everything seemed delicious, but after a while Caroline wasn't so sure—maybe her mother was right. The smell was a little overpowering. Rae was struggling with the basket, so Caroline took a side. "It's okay, I'm over it. Not hungry anymore. Isn't it weird how mostly everything on a stick is deep fried?"

Rae nodded and pointed to the bottom of the basket. It was soaked with oil.

••••

When the hour was up, Caroline and Rae went back to the tent and lined up their samples on a table. There was a deep-fried Twinkie on a stick, deep-fried cereal on a stick, deep-fried peanut butter pickle on a stick, deep-fried corn on the cob on a stick, deep-fried bacon-wrapped turkey leg on a stick, deep-fried Oreo on a stick, deep-fried cheese on a stick, deep-fried brownie on a stick, deep-fried lasagna on a stick, deep-fried wontons on a stick, grilled shrimp on a stick, a candy apple on a stick, and finally, cotton candy on a stick.

Rae wasn't sure about the cotton candy. Was that really a food?

Oliver and Tate had an impressive collection too. They added them to the table. Lined up in a row, the foods on a stick did not look delicious. They looked brown, greasy, and disgusting.

"Attention, junior chefs!" Chef Gary raised his arms. "We have a twist to this challenge." Everyone froze. "You will not be using a deep fryer in this challenge because . . . Can anyone tell me why?"

Tate waved his hand. "Because all the deep-fried stuff has already been invented."

Chef Gary laughed. "True, but not the right answer."

Oliver gave a try. "Excuse me, Chef, but is it because it's not heart-healthy?"

"Yes!" Chef Gary held up the deep-fried Oreo on a stick. "A good chef makes food to nourish the body. Is this good for your body?"

"NO, CHEF!"

"CUT!" shouted Steve.

"What?" Tate looked confused. "Aren't we starting the challenge?"

Chef Nancy pointed to a table at the back of the tent. "We'll continue with the challenge after lunch. Let's go eat. We have sandwiches and salads. You must be starving."

Rae leaned over to Caroline. "I'm not. Are you?"

Caroline shook her head. "All I can smell is greasy food."

CHAPTER 24

hirty minutes later, the cameras were rolling and Tate, Rae, Caroline, and Oliver were lined up in front of the workstations, ready with aprons on.

Chef Gary looked them over. This was serious—no one smiled. "The challenge I'm giving you today is to make a non-deep-fried savory snack on a stick. Do you understand?"

"YES, CHEF!"

"You'll have five minutes in the pantry and then forty minutes to cook. Your time starts now!"

Everyone raced to the pantry. Of course they were nervous, but not about forgetting anything. They each had a list taped to the inside bottom of their basket, where the cameras couldn't see it. That was a trick of the show. Five minutes wasn't a lot of time in the pantry. It helped that they had done some practicing.

"TIME!" called Chef Gary. "Back to your workstations."

"CUT!" yelled Steve. Everyone stopped and ran back, but instead of unpacking and starting to work, they put their baskets on their tables and waited. This was another trick of the show. The cameras turned off—this part would not be on TV. Chef Nancy walked to each workstation to visit and go over cooking strategies. She offered up suggestions, too.

"Caroline, get those profiteroles into the oven as fast as possible. They'll need to cool before you add your fillings."

"Oliver, if you moisten your crispy chip in the very center, you'll be able to skewer it without breaking it apart."

"Rae, you'll need a crispy crust on the corn cake to keep it on the stick, and try to keep them small, or they'll be heavy."

"Tate, you'll want your sauce to stick to the meatball. Try for a thick mayonnaise consistency, and use a squeeze bottle for visual effect."

Once Chef Nancy was done, Steve gave the signal for the cameras to turn back on. Chef Gary walked to the center of the room, raised his hand, and shouted, "Let's get cooking!"

Suddenly the tent was bustling with activity.

Chef Aimee and Chef Gary visited the contestants while they worked.

Rae blanched three ears of corn, cut off the kernels, and dropped them into a hot pan. She shook the pan, flipping the kernels from the back to the front.

Chef Aimee watched. "Nice pan skills! What's next?"

Rae didn't look up—she was too focused. "I'm frying the

corn cakes with bacon fat to give them a crispy glaze. I'll put them on my skewer between slices of crispy pork belly."

"Sounds delicious—I like the variations in textures. Nicely done!"

Rae looked up and smiled. A compliment from Chef Aimee was worth stopping for.

"What's cooking, Tate?" It was Chef Gary. "I hear you're something of an inventor."

Tate nodded. "I like to make my own recipes and try new combinations. I'm making Afghan lamb meatballs with a spicy Korean Gochujang yogurt sauce and crispy rice bites."

"Sweet, spicy, savory—you've got a lot going on there. I like the fusion of cuisines; it's interesting. Can't wait to taste it." Chef Gary tapped the table. "Keep up the energy—you have a lot to do."

Tate chopped his onion at lightning speed. He didn't look up, but he hoped Chef Gary and the cameras were watching.

Oliver knew how to make steak: salt, pepper, and then a two-minute sear per side for a perfect medium rare. He was making steak bites with blue cheese butter and a sprinkling of crushed walnuts for crunch.

"And to accompany it?" asked Chef Gary.

Oliver picked up a potato. "Frites would've been perfect, but since I can't use the deep fryer, I'm improvising."

Chef Gary nodded. "Great things can come out of improvisation."

"Yes, sir." Oliver picked up a mandolin and started to thinly slice the potato. "I'll flavor these with garlic, stick them in the broiler, then finish them off with a dusting of dried olives and sea salt."

"Good work," said Chef Gary. "And by the way, that sounds much better than a french fry."

Caroline was a mess: she was white as meringue, and flour was everywhere.

Chef Aimee rushed over to help. "What happened?"

Caroline was almost in tears. "The flour bag ripped and now there's too much flour in my bowl. My profiteroles are ruined. And there isn't time to make more!"

Chef Aimee looked at her watch. "Thirty minutes left. Can you change gears? Make something different? Take a minute and look over your ingredients."

Caroline's workstation was covered with flour. The butter, the eggs, the milk . . .

"CREPES!" shouted Caroline. She threw up her arms. A cloud of flour engulfed her.

Chef Aimee jumped back.

"I CAN MAKE CREPES!"

"Yes!" Chef Aimee smiled and brushed off her dress. "You sure can! Now get cooking!"

CHAPTER 25

ime was up. Eight hands were in the air.

"Hands down," said Chef Gary. "Please bring your skewers to the front. We can't wait to see what you've made."

I made three spicy mini corn cakes to go with my crispy garlic pork belly. The corn cakes are inspired by the flavors of Mexican street corn. My neighbor Mrs. Ramez makes the best elotes! I used chili powder for spice, cheese for creaminess, and lime to add just a bit of tartness.

RAE

OLIVER

I made steak bites with a topping of blue cheese butter and a sprinkling of crushed walnuts and parsley. Not everyone can cook a steak to perfection. I learned from the best. Each bite is paired with crispy potato chips dusted with salt and dried olives. That way you get the meaty taste of the steak and the salty crunch of the chip.

I made crepe dumplings. It was a last-minute change. Crepes have always been one of my favorites. My mom showed me how to make them. Each skewer has three different cheesy dumplings. There's brie and sweet pepper jelly, cheddar and apple compote, and goat cheese and basil.

CAROLINE

TATE

I made Afghan lamb meatballs drizzled with a spicy Korean Gochujang yogurt sauce and crispy rice bites. My dad inspires my cooking, with his travels in the army. He introduces me to foods from different countries. I just put them together in my own way.

When everyone was done presenting, Chef Gary made an announcement. "We have another surprise. Your challenge is not over. Chef Aimee and I are not going to be the judges of this challenge." He paused. "We're going to let the people at this fair vote for the winner."

Caroline looked at Rae, Rae looked at Oliver, and Oliver and Tate both shrugged. They were all confused.

Chef Gary turned to the back of the tent. "Will our helper chefs please come out to the front!"

Eight chefs in matching aprons marched out from behind a curtain and stood next to Chef Gary.

"These chefs are going to help you make fifty duplicates of the skewer you just presented. Then we'll have fifty people here at the fair try each of your skewers and vote on their favorite. The one with the most votes will be the winner. You'll each have two helper chefs and two hours to finish this challenge. Can you do it?"

"Yes, Chef!"

Rae shouted too. But was it true? Could they really do it?

It's not really fair. If I knew that we were presenting to the people at the fair I would have made something different. I'm not sure that a person who likes a deep-fried Oreo is going to be a good judge of steak bites with blue cheese and walnuts.

OLIVER

....

Rae felt lucky. Her helper chefs, Raymond and Phoebe, were amazing, and they had good ideas about how to make the process go faster. It had taken her forty minutes to make just one skewer. Making fifty seemed almost impossible.

"Division of labor," said Phoebe. "If we each concentrate on one thing, it'll save time."

Phoebe prepped the corn and helped Rae make the corn cakes. Raymond handled the pork belly. When all the ingredients were ready, they worked together to assemble the skewers.

CAROLINE

I've never made so many crepes in my life. It's a good thing they're easy to make. I can't even count how many times we had to go back to the pantry to get more eggs. I'm pretty much an expert at crepes now. My skewer was the most challenging, because each crepe dumpling has a different filling. If I knew we were going to have to make fifty of them, I might have made something different, but definitely not profiteroles. That would have been even more work.

Gochujang sauce is strong. You have to be careful. Devon, one of my helper chefs, rubbed his nose and got some next to his eye. The medic had to take him away for ten minutes to fix it. Ten minutes without a helper is a big deal if you're in a competition, but we got a surprise. Chef Gary came and took Devon's place. It was amazing. I got to cook right next to Chef Gary!

TATE

CHAPTER 26

A tasting area was roped off outside the tent for the judging. Tate snuck a peek. The helper chefs were setting up the skewers on four numbered tables. Which one was his? He couldn't tell. He looked to the left. A long line of people stood waiting to get in. Caroline crept behind Tate to have a look. The first thing she noticed was the stage with the microphones and, of course, cameras. She scratched her arm. Now she wished she hadn't looked.

Chef Gary called everyone to the middle of the tent. "Junior chefs, may I have your attention! Here's what's going to happen. I'm going outside to introduce the challenge." Chef Gary pointed toward the tasting area. "And then after that we'll bring you out to meet the fair attendees who will be judging your food. Just step forward and wave when I call your name, and then once that's done, you can come back here to relax. That was a busy two hours. You deserve a rest!

The helper chefs will be in charge of handing out the skewers and the voting cards."

Tate, Oliver, Caroline, and Rae stood in the tent, waiting for Chef Nancy's signal. Chef Gary and Chef Aimee were outside talking to the fairgoers. Everyone loved Chef Gary; he knew how to make an audience laugh.

And here they are, our four young junior chefs! And one of them will be the Next Best Junior Chef!

"Go," whispered Chef Nancy.

Tate, Oliver, Caroline, and Rae ran out of the tent.

CAROLINE

> There were so many people, I thought I'd be nervous, but I wasn't. It made me feel like a superstar, especially when Chef Gary said my name and everyone clapped.

....

After the introductions, Chef Nancy welcomed them back into the tent. "Enjoy yourselves, and relax. I'm so proud of you. You all did a great job today!" She pointed to the back of the tent. "I have a few calls to make. I'll be right over there if you need me."

Rae sat down, stood up, sat down, then stood up again. "I can't relax! People are eating my food right now! And they're grading me! What if they don't like it?"

Oliver stood up. "What if they love it?"

"Exactly!" Tate jumped on a chair and struck a pose. "My, my—this is delightful. In fact, it's delightfulness . . . ON A STICK!!"

Soon they were all shouting out suggestions.

"Deliciousness . . . ON A STICK!"

"Lusciousness . . . ON A STICK!"

"Tastiness . . . ON A STICK!"

Chef Nancy rushed over, arms waving. "SHHHHHH! SHHHHH! SHHHH!!!! They'll hear you outside!"

Getting in trouble was worth it; they collapsed into their chairs. No one was nervous anymore.

Everyone stood up the second they saw Chef Gary come back into the tent. This was it, the big announcement. Rae crossed her fingers for luck, but instead of announcing the winner, Chef Gary announced something else.

"While Chef Aimee oversees the counting of the votes, we'd like you to do a quick round of interviews."

Caroline groaned, then quickly covered her mouth. Luckily Chef Gary didn't hear her—he was gone again.

I'm going to win because my skewer is a sweet and spicy taste of summer.

RAE

OLIVER

I'm going to win because my skewer is sophisticated and homey.

I'm going to win because my skewer is a sampling of three different tastes.

CAROLINE

I'm going to win because my skewer is daring and challenging for the tongue.

TATE

....

When Chef Gary came back the second time, Chef Aimee was with him, and so were the camerapeople.

"This is it!" whispered Rae.

Caroline squeezed her hand. "Good luck!"

Chef Gary looked at each of them and smiled. "Junior chefs, you have managed to do something that chefs twice your age rarely do. This was a taste of what it's like to work in a real restaurant, and you succeeded. Congratulations to all of you! But as you know, every competition has only one winner."

Chef Aimee stepped forward. "The votes have been tallied. Congratulations, Oliver! You are the winner of this challenge. Your recipe was clean, simple, and classic, but with an edge. The blue cheese and walnut compote was an inspired addition, as were the seasoned chips. Sometimes less is more, and you demonstrated this perfectly."

Chef Gary clapped his hands. "Well done, Oliver!"

They all clapped, and Oliver bounced up and down just like Tate.

Chef Aimee put her arm around his shoulder. "Now comes my favorite part. Oliver, since you are the winner, you get to choose a gadget and the fate of Chef Gary. I want you to think hard about this: pie in the face or Jell-O dunk tank?"

Everyone screamed out suggestions.

"Dunk tank!"

"Pie in the face!"

"Dunk tank!"

Oliver whispered something to Chef Aimee. She held up her hand. "JELL-O DUNK TANK it is!"

They all screamed again, but this time it was because Chef Gary was standing behind Oliver wearing a bathing suit and a snorkel.

A dunk tank was wheeled out and Chef Gary climbed up onto the seat. Rae wondered if Chef Gary already knew about the Jell-O color, because it matched his green bathing suit perfectly.

Oliver got to go first. Chef Gary didn't stand a chance. Oliver's arm was as good for throwing as it was for catching.

The ball smashed against the target, ringing the bell, and a surprised Chef Gary dropped straight into the Jell-O.

Chef Gary got dunked two more times. His only lucky break was Caroline. She had horrible aim. She couldn't get the ball anywhere close to the target. That was too bad—Tate really wanted to see Chef Gary get dunked one more time.

CHAPTER 27

Rae followed Caroline to the breakfast buffet. Caroline grabbed a bowl and a spoon, then stopped, motionless, in front of the cereal display.

Rae gave her a nudge. "What's up? You stuck?"

Caroline pointed the spoon. "Sort of. I'm tired of eating cereal, but if I lose tomorrow and have to go home, that means today and tomorrow are my last chance to have any. You know my mom—no junk food allowed!"

Rae wasn't expecting that. Caroline going home was not something she wanted to think about. In fact, she didn't want to think about anyone going home.

Oliver was in a great mood. He held up a hand blender. "My pick from the Gadget Wall. I didn't get a chance to put it in my toolbox yet." He put it on the table.

All during breakfast he joked with Caroline, smiled at Rae, and tossed an apple back and forth with Tate. But Rae didn't trust the carefree happiness. Oliver wasn't the kind of person who'd forget about camera cards. She'd have to be extra careful. There was a whole day where something could go wrong. If she lost a card they'd be tied, and then what? He wanted that private lesson as much as she did.

Chef Nancy came into the room wearing a sun hat. "We will be spending the day on Porter Farm, and Chef Porter has some nice treats in store for us."

No one cheered. Chef Nancy knew why. They were scared of Chef Porter. She couldn't blame them; Chef Porter was intimidating—and a famous world-class chef. She'd just have to work harder to get them excited. "I'll be giving you a tour of the farm this morning, and then Chef Porter will meet you for a lunchtime surprise."

"Oooh." Caroline and Rae both nodded.

Surprise was a good word. It energized people.

Chef Nancy continued. "There will be cameras following us today, so be mindful. But today is not about competition—it's about fun. We're going to enjoy the experience, enjoy each other, and rest up for tomorrow."

Rae waved her hand. "Does that mean I won the private lesson?"

Chef Nancy shook her head. "We'll have to wait until the end of the day for that one." Rae slumped and Oliver stood taller. He still had a chance.

Porter Farm was right next door, an easy walk.

Chef Nancy led the way. "Our first stop will be the herb garden."

Caroline stepped up next to Rae and bumped her play-fully. The cameras followed closely behind. Chef Nancy was right. When they were out and walking around, she hardly even noticed them. Of course, cameras at the workstation were different, but today she didn't have to think about any of that.

She turned to Oliver. "If you were sitting in the dunk tank, what would you want to fall into?"

Oliver paused. That wasn't such an easy question. He had favorites, but there were other factors to consider. Ice cream was delicious, but it would be cold and hard. Crème brûlée wasn't good either, because of the burnt-sugar crust. He finally chose vanilla milkshake: ice cream but runny. He'd just have to deal with the cold.

"Cotton candy," said Tate.

Rae nodded. That was a good one.

Caroline held up her hand. "Crème pâtissière."

Rae nodded again. "Yum! Who doesn't like pastry cream?"

"What about you?" Caroline nudged her.

Rae's favorite thing was not perfect for the dunk tank, but she said it anyway. "Guacamole!"

CHAPTER 28

The herb garden was a hit with everyone, especially Rae. It was exciting to see the herbs she cooked with in their natural environment. Chef Nancy let them pick parsley, basil, thyme, chervil, tarragon, chives, dill, mint, oregano, rosemary, sage, and cilantro. Then she showed them nasturtiums, which are flowers you can eat.

Caroline picked a mint leaf and sucked on it. "Sweet and a little tangy!"

"Not this one." Tate waved a cilantro sprig.

"Ew." Caroline covered her nose. "Soap!"

After the herbs, they walked over to the chickens. Chef Nancy quickened her step. She had a feeling this was going to be a highlight.

"Really? We get to pick eggs?" Tate was excited.

Caroline shook her head. "Not pick, gather. Eggs don't grow on trees."

Tate didn't care about terminology. He ran ahead and waited at the gate.

The chicken area was fenced off to keep the chickens in and predators out.

"Unfortunately," said Chef Nancy, "it isn't just people who think chickens are tasty."

Chef Nancy opened the gate. "Chef Porter loves her chickens, so no running in here, and be respectful of the animals. The eggs are in the coop. You may collect an egg, but only if there isn't a chicken sitting on it. And please bring them back one at a time. We don't want to break any."

The chicken coop was huge; there was plenty of room for everyone to stand. There were three levels of shelves, each divided into little boxes.

"Look!" said Caroline. "They each have their own bedroom!"

"Pretty skimpy bedrooms," said Oliver. Once a chicken was sitting in the box, there wasn't much extra room on the sides.

Rae shot him a look. "Bigger is not always better." Back home her own bedroom was small—just big enough for her bed and one dresser.

Caroline was the first to find an egg. "I got a brown one! And it's warm!" That was a surprise. Suddenly the egg seemed more precious. She was extra careful carrying it out to Chef Nancy.

Soon everyone was finding eggs in beautiful shades of brown and cream. Oliver was in the coop next to Rae when he spotted it. A blue egg! He reached in front of her, but then stopped himself. What if he let Rae get it? Maybe if she was extra excited and happy, she'd forget about the camera cards. That was the only way he'd win. She would only make a mistake if her guard was down.

"OLIVER! Really? There's the whole coop and you have to be right in front of me?" Rae pushed past him angrily, and then she saw it. A blue egg! Why hadn't Oliver taken it? Was it a message? His way of saying *Forget the competition—let's just have fun*? She took the egg out to Chef Nancy. If Oliver was being nice, she could be nice too. She'd try harder.

"A blue egg?" Tate couldn't believe it.

Chef Nancy carefully placed it in the basket with the other eggs. "Isn't it beautiful? This is from a special breed of chicken called an Ameraucana."

Rae started to nod, then stopped and stared. Her mouth dropped open. Chef Porter was heading straight toward her, and there was a chicken riding on her shoulder.

CHAPTER 29

Everyone gathered around Chef Porter.

Chef Nancy put her finger to her lips. "Quiet voices, please. See, I told you. Chef Porter loves her chickens."

Tate was shocked. This couldn't be the same person who'd frowned at him in the filming studio. Chef Porter smiled and introduced the chicken

"Good morning, junior chefs. I see you've been busy." She pointed to the basket of eggs. "My friend here is very special." Chef Porter tickled the chicken's neck with her finger. "This is Nancy. She's two years old and a special breed of chicken called a Belgian bearded d'Uccle bantam."

That was a long name. Tate hoped there wouldn't be a test. Nancy was easier to remember. Could chickens be pretty?

If so, Nancy was beautiful. She had rust-colored feathers speckled with black and white dots, and they covered her feet like fancy feathered boots.

Tate raised his hand. "Is her name Nancy because of Chef Nancy?"

Chef Porter shook her head. "Good question, Tate, but no. This Nancy is named after a great inventor, Nancy M. Johnson. Do you know what she invented?"

Tate shook his head. He was pretty surprised Chef Porter knew his name.

"Nancy M. Johnson invented the first hand-cranked ice cream maker over one hundred and fifty years ago, in 1843. It was revolutionary, and made ice cream easier to make. Can you imagine a world without ice cream?" Chef Porter shook her head. "I can't. I love ice cream, so my Nancy is named in honor of Nancy M. Johnson."

The kids were trying hard not to laugh. Nancy the chicken was pecking at Chef Porter's head, but Chef Porter didn't seem to mind. She just put her hand up and stroked Nancy's feathers.

"Nancy can be naughty. It's in her genes. Did you know that chickens are the closest living relatives to the *Tyrannosaurus rex*?"

Everyone nodded. They all knew that.

Chef Nancy handed the basket of eggs to Chef Porter. "Thank you, Chef Porter, for letting us visit with your chickens. We'll see you soon, at lunch?"

Chef Porter nodded and Nancy the chicken jiggled up and down on her shoulder. "I'm looking forward to it. We're going to cook up these beautiful fresh eggs." Chef Porter handed the basket over to a helper, and then she and Nancy headed back down the path.

Chef Nancy pointed in the opposite direction. "Next stop, the restaurant. We'll take the scenic route." The restaurant was on top of a small bluff overlooking the fields, the lodge, and the filming studios. It was famous and very popular; it took months just to get a reservation. Lunchtime with Chef Porter was definitely a special treat.

Tate ran ahead, then collapsed on the ground in a fit of giggles. He didn't know why, but a chicken riding on Chef Porter's shoulder was the funniest thing he'd ever seen. What if Nancy the chicken had suddenly turned into a mini *T. rex*? That would have been a surprise—for everyone! When the group caught up, he was still rolling around laughing.

Chef Nancy decided it was a good time for a rest, so they all sat down to enjoy the view.

Rae studied Chef Nancy. "Are you named after the ice cream inventor too?"

"No, I'm named after my great-aunt Nancy. She didn't invent anything, but my mother loved her very much."

Tate nodded. "Well, that's better than being named after a chicken."

After that, there were five minutes of chicken jokes. None of them was very good, but everyone laughed. It felt good to let off steam. Rae thought of a new joke, but she didn't share it. *Why did the chicken cross the road? She was eliminated from the challenge.* After tomorrow, things would be different. One of them would be gone.

Chef Nancy stood up. "Okay, break is over. Let's go make some lunch!"

CHAPTER 30

Everything was ready and waiting for them in the restaurant kitchen when they arrived. Chef Porter was wearing an apron and was standing behind a long table. Across from her was a workstation set up with cutting boards, knives, bowls, utensils, and aprons. Nancy the chicken was not on her shoulder. Chef Porter didn't like to waste time; as soon as the aprons were on, she got started.

"Today we are going to make a fine herb omelet with the eggs from my hens and the herbs from my garden. As young chefs, you know the first step is always to prepare your ingredients. Please chop the herbs in front of you. You will need one half tablespoon of parsley, chervil, chives, and tarragon."

Tate grabbed the knife and started chopping. He liked Chef Porter a lot more when she was just giving directions.

Once the herbs were done, Chef Porter continued. "Crack

your eggs and add a splash of water. The water will encourage your omelet to be light and fluffy."

Rae noticed something right away. Fresh eggs cracked differently than store-bought eggs. The shells stayed together better, plus the yolks were super yellow. She almost said something, but Chef Porter wasn't the kind of person you interrupted. Rae held the blue egg and nudged Caroline. Would it be different inside? Caroline stopped cracking and watched. Rae tapped the shell and pulled the egg open. A bright yellow yolk fell into the bowl. It was disappointing, but only slightly. A blue omelet would be weird. The shell was so pretty. Could she keep it? And then for no reason other than happiness, she held up the shell and smiled, and there right in front of her was a camera pointed right at her face. NO! It was only a second, but it changed everything.

Rae held her breath, waiting, but nothing happened. Chef Nancy did not march over and ask for a camera card. If no one saw, did it count? Maybe the cameraperson wouldn't tell.

Chef Porter continued with the instructions. "Bring your bowls and follow me to the stoves." There was a large bank of stoves with tools laid out. Chef Porter grabbed a skillet and placed it on the burner.

"Heat the skillet on medium heat, add the butter, and when it is no longer foaming you may add your eggs. Gently scrape the bottom of the pan with a plastic spatula to allow the liquid egg mixture to run under the egg that has already set. Once your eggs are completely set you may add the fine herbs."

Rae was frantic but pretending to be calm. She scanned the room. Chef Nancy was in the distance watching. Would she come over to get a card? Rae couldn't concentrate. Her omelet was brown and lopsided. Hopefully Chef Porter wouldn't notice. She covered it with her spatula.

Oliver was an omelet expert. The end part was his favorite. Fold twice and tilt. His omelet slid onto the plate with the folded edges down. "Perfect!"

Chef Porter didn't stay for the eating part. Chef Nancy apologized: "Chef Porter is sorry she can't be here, but she has a very busy schedule. It takes a lot of work to run this farm."

No one minded. Especially Rae.

The omelets were delicious, but Rae ate slowly. Her appetite was gone. Should she tell? Was it cheating not to? What about Oliver?

Caroline scraped her plate clean. "Fresh eggs taste so much better!"

Tate held up his fork. "Thank you, chickens."

....

After lunch, Chef Nancy led everyone to the back of the room. There were two baskets on the table: an empty one and a basket filled with fresh vegetables.

"These vegetables are from the gardens at Porter Farm. They were gathered this morning. Chef Porter has generously offered them to us for the elimination challenge."

Everyone stood at attention.

"Oliver, since you won the last challenge you may go first. Please choose a fresh vegetable to take back to the filming studio to use in tomorrow's elimination challenge." Chef Nancy pointed to the empty basket. "You may put it in there."

Rae couldn't believe it. Knowing an ingredient ahead of time was a huge advantage, for all of them. It meant they'd have time to prepare and think about creative recipes.

Oliver looked at Rae and scowled. She knew why. This was it. He thought the race was over and she was the winner, but was she? Wasn't it still a tie? She should say something, tell Chef Nancy, but she didn't. Instead, she looked at her feet. Oliver picked four sweet potatoes and walked toward the empty basket.

Caroline nodded. Versatile choice, but maybe too safe. Sweet potatoes were easy to cook and the judges would know that. Her thoughts were interrupted—Oliver's potatoes were suddenly rolling all over the floor. Oliver dropped to his knees and snatched three, but the fourth rolled under the table. He scooted on his stomach, then emerged potato in hand, smiling for the camera.

Rae gasped and covered her mouth. Camera card! And obviously he'd done it on purpose.

Oliver looked at her and shrugged.

Chef Nancy said nothing. Instead, she continued with the vegetables. "We'll choose the remaining order out of a hat to be fair." She pulled off her hat, dumped three pieces of paper in it, then pulled them out again and read off the names—Tate, Caroline, then Rae. Tate picked red and yellow beets, Caroline picked baby eggplants, and Rae picked poblano peppers.

I picked baby eggplants because they have an earthy flavor and a comforting texture. I'd like to pair them with something like a roast or duck.

CAROLINE

TATE

I picked beets because they have a rich texture and great color. I might make a goat cheese and beet tart to accompany beef or lamb.

OLIVER

I picked sweet potatoes because they are a transformation vegetable. You can use them for anything. I could make an almond wasabi-crusted potato pancake to go with braised pork roast.

I picked poblano peppers because I love to add heat to my dishes. The poblano pepper will be great in a side dish like spicy mac and cheese or spicy pilaf with raisins and nuts.

RAE

••••

As soon as the vegetables were chosen and the cameras were off, Tate ran up to Oliver.

"Did you smile on purpose?"

Oliver shrugged. "Maybe. What's the difference? The game's over. Rae has all her cards. She won. It doesn't matter anymore."

Except that Oliver was wrong. It did.

CHAPTER 31

That evening, after the video-chats with their families, Chef Nancy gathered everyone together.

She held up a camera card. "It's time to announce a winner, but first I need to collect a few remaining camera cards. Rae, will you please hand me a card?"

"WHAT?" Oliver stared at Chef Nancy, then at Rae.

Rae was blushing.

Chef Nancy walked over to Rae. "Did you smile at the camera this afternoon while we were cooking with Chef Porter?"

Rae nodded and handed Chef Nancy a camera card.

"Oliver, will you please hand me a camera card?"

Oliver's face was red too, but not from embarrassment. "Wait a minute, ma'am! You mean we were tied? I HAD A CHANCE TO BE THE WINNER? That's not fair. Ma'am, if I knew that, I would never have dropped the potatoes!"

Tate gasped. "You dropped the potatoes on purpose? Why?"

Oliver brushed him off. "Camera time, but it doesn't matter."

Chef Nancy scowled. "Yes, it does matter. The purpose of the camera cards is to moderate your actions in front of the camera. Dropping the potatoes to get more time on film is both sneaky and manipulative. Please hand me two cards. One for dropping the potatoes and one for smiling."

"Not fair," grumbled Oliver, but he handed over the cards.

Chef Nancy walked back to the center of the room. "After tallying each contestant's camera card count, the winner of the private lesson is Rae, with nine cards remaining."

No one clapped or said anything. They were all too uncomfortable. Minutes later Tate, Oliver, and Caroline headed over to the library to do some research for their dishes.

Rae followed Chef Nancy to the school studio. Chef Nancy tried to reassure her. "It was fair and square. This was a game against the cards, not each other."

····

The school studio was dark. Chef Nancy turned the lights on, but it felt strange and empty without the other kids or the camera crew.

Chef Nancy walked to Rae's workstation. "So, what are we doing? What would you like to learn about?"

Rae looked at the floor. Her face was red again—she could feel it.

Chef Nancy led Rae to a chair. "Do you feel faint? Sit down. It's okay. Take your time. You can ask me anything."

Rae pointed to the food processor. "I don't know how to use it. Can you teach me?"

Chef Nancy was surprised, then embarrassed. It was her job to train all the contestants and she'd failed. She hadn't gone over the basics. Not everyone had the same tools at home.

Chef Nancy pulled the food processor out and put it on the counter. "Let's do it!"

Rae was a good student. In less than an hour, she had mastered the food processor and all of its accessories.

••••

That night before falling asleep, Rae told Caroline about the blue egg. "He let me have it on purpose, just so I would think he's nice. Which he isn't, obviously."

Caroline nodded. "I guess so. I still can't believe he dropped those potatoes on purpose just to get more time on TV. Why? I didn't want to be filmed when I dropped my strawberries."

Rae shrugged. "I don't know. Maybe he wants to be a chef and a TV star. He's tricky. We have to watch out for him."

CHAPTER 32

The interviews in the morning went well—maybe too well. Oliver was worried. It all seemed a little too easy. Tate thought so too. The final challenge was supposed to be tough. Why were they given an ingredient ahead of time? Rae and Caroline didn't seem worried—they were more concerned about seeing their parents. The parents were invited to the filming of the elimination round. Oliver made sure his shirt was tucked in extra neatly—his mom was coming. She cared about stuff like that.

Chef Nancy went over the schedule. "You'll have fifteen minutes with your parents and then we'll move to the back room for a special talk."

Rae wasn't looking forward to the visit. It would've been different if her grandma was coming too, but she had a bad hip and couldn't sit in the car for long trips, so it was just going to be her dad. They didn't have a lot in common, especially food. Her dad was a burger and pizza kind of guy, and he put ketchup on almost everything.

Caroline was feeling like Rae, but for different reasons. Her mom made her nervous. No matter how good a chef she tried to be, her mom would always be better. It wasn't easy to follow perfection.

Once Chef Nancy had approved of everyone's outfit, she led them to the room to meet their parents. Like usual, Tate was first to the door, but then he stopped right in the doorway. Rae bumped into him, but he didn't move. A man in an army uniform was kneeling on the floor: Tate's dad. Everyone watched. Tate screamed and ran into his arms.

Rae found her dad. He hugged her twice, once because he was happy to see her, and an extra time for her grandma.

Oliver's mom straightened his shirt, even though he was pretty sure it was already perfect. "Nice choice. It brings out the green in your eyes."

Oliver nodded.

His mom gave him a hug. "I miss your pasta alla pescatore."

He hugged her back. Their language was food.

Caroline told her mom about the eggplant—that was a mistake. Suddenly her mom was full of recipe ideas and tips: *baked eggplant chips, roasted ratatouille tart, remember to salt and pat it dry, it's very good if you roast it, don't use oil in the pan to fry it or it will get mushy* . . . Caroline's head was spinning when she finally hugged her goodbye.

Tate couldn't let go. That wasn't just a saying. It was fact. His mom and Chef Nancy had to pry him away from his dad. Tate wiped his eyes.

His dad had been crying too. "It's okay, little buddy. I'll be right here when you get back."

CHAPTER 33

hef Nancy had memorized her special talk, but now she couldn't remember how it started. The parent meeting had been surprisingly emotional; it had thrown her off-course. All she had were bits and pieces: *never give up, do your best, have a plan, there are no losers . . .* It wasn't anything new. She'd said it all before. She gave up on it and instead suggested they each share a wish with the group. The kids were surprised, but willing.

"I wish you calmness," offered Oliver. "So you don't get nervous."

"I wish you planning," added Rae. "So you don't run out of time."

"I wish you creativity," said Tate. "So you make something great."

Caroline held up her hands. "I wish you steadiness, so you don't make mistakes."

Chef Nancy stepped forward with her arms open wide. "And I wish you joy, so you all have fun."

They all joined together in their first-ever group hug.

••••

"TIME!" Steve rapped on the door.

Chef Nancy pulled away from the group. "Okay. This is it. Let's go line up at the door."

It was the same line as the first day, but it felt different. This time they were going in as a team.

"Rolling!" shouted Steve.

"*Next Best Junior Chef* is proud to invite our four junior chefs to the first elimination round of this competition. Please welcome Caroline, Tate, Oliver, and Rae."

This wasn't like last time. Rae enjoyed every minute of the walk to the front of the room.

Chef Gary stepped forward. "Welcome, junior chefs. Are you ready for your challenge?"

"YES, CHEF!"

He held up a basket. "Our junior chefs have each picked a fresh vegetable from Chef Porter's farm to use in today's elimination challenge."

He handed out the vegetables. "Sweet potatoes for Oliver, red and yellow beets for Tate, baby eggplants for Caroline, and poblano peppers for Rae. Wow! I bet you've all been researching recipes."

The kids mumbled and nodded.

"Chef Aimee, can you please come forward and show our young chefs what you've made?"

Chef Aimee smiled and presented her plate. "It's a beautiful candied mushroom tartlette . . . for dessert!"

Tate and Oliver both groaned. Tate because he was worried, and Oliver because of the mushrooms.

Chef Gary smiled. "That's right—we want you to be magicians. We want you to turn those vegetables into desserts."

Now everyone else groaned too.

"I knew it," whispered Oliver. "They tricked us." But it didn't make him feel any better.

Chef Porter stepped forward. "I can't wait to see what you do with my beautiful vegetables. You'll have ninety minutes to create a dessert. Do you accept this challenge?"

There was only one answer.

"Yes, Chef!"

Chef Gary waved his arm. "Let's get cooking!"

Everyone ran to the workstations.

"Cut," called Steve. The cameras stopped rolling.

There wasn't time for talking—only for thinking. Chef Nancy gave them each pens and papers to make a pantry list. In ten minutes the cameras would be back on. That wasn't a lot of time to plan a dessert.

Of course I was shocked. I'm not a magician. But then I remembered my neighbor Mrs. Demir. If she can make dessert pudding out of a chicken, I can make dessert out of poblano peppers. The trick was to think of a dessert that could be sweet and spicy.

RAE

OLIVER

My first thought was *YES! I got this!* It's easy to make a dessert out of sweet potatoes, but then that's the problem. It's too easy. I'm going to have to use extra creativity to win this and wow the judges.

Yes, I was pretty surprised about the switch, but I was more surprised that I got an idea of what to make right away. That's never happened to me before. It felt great.

CAROLINE

TATE

It was a big surprise, but today's been a day for big surprises. I'm having trouble concentrating. Beets have a sweetness to them. I'm lucky. I can use that.

CHAPTER 34

"Rolling!" shouted Steve.

Chef Gary stepped to the center of the room. "Do you know what you're going to make? Are you ready to start?"

"Yes, Chef!"

"You'll have ten minutes in the pantry to pick out your ingredients."

Chef Gary raised his hand. "GO!"

Everyone rushed into the pantry. It was the quietest pantry run ever. Not even Rae was talking.

"And, time!" called Chef Gary.

"And, cut!" shouted Steve.

····

Chef Nancy had five minutes with each contestant before the cameras started again. She listened to their ideas and helped them plan out their strategies. She had only one goal—she wanted everyone to do their very best.

"Oliver, that ice cream needs to be made as fast as possible so you can get it into the freezer."

"Tate, get those beets in the oven, but remember to leave out two so they can be candied."

"Caroline, caramelize the apples and eggplant first, then prepare your pastry."

"Rae, roast and then liquefy those peppers in the food processor."

Rae nodded and smiled. She knew exactly how to do it.

····

"And, rolling!" shouted Steve.

Chef Gary walked to the center of the room and raised his hand, then brought it down hard. "Let's get cooking!"

This was it! The race was on. Chef Nancy had three wishes for every challenge: that no one drop anything, that no one burn anything, and that no one cut themselves. She crossed her fingers. It might not help, but at this point it was all she could do. For the next seventy-five minutes, the kids were on their own.

Rae was starting with the hot pepper brittle. It was the fiery crunch that would contrast with the creamy smoothness of her mango pie. Brittle wasn't so different from the filling of baklava. She put sugar and corn syrup into a pot and brought it to a boil. When the sugar was dissolved, she added piñon nuts.

Chef Aimee stopped by to visit with Caroline. Caroline liked the attention, but it was hard to cook and talk at the same time.

"Oooh," said Chef Aimee. "What smells so good?"

Caroline pointed to the caramelized apples. "I just finished those up, and now I'm caramelizing the baby eggplants." A thin layer of sliced eggplants nested in a froth of butter and sugar.

Chef Aimee took one more sniff. "Yum! Keep it up."

Caroline was relieved when Chef Aimee left. There was still a lot to do. Now was not a time for chitchatting. Next up was the pastry cream.

Oliver felt bad about using the microwave; he was old-fashioned. Normally he would have baked the sweet potatoes, but there wasn't time for that. He needed them cooked fast. While he was waiting for the bell on the timer, he made the ice cream base, adding vanilla, cinnamon, and cream cheese for tanginess, then rushing it to the fridge to cool.

Chef Gary came over to talk just as Oliver was pouring his mixture into the ice cream maker. This was Oliver's favorite part. He turned the handle and waited for the ice cream to ooze out.

"What's the flavor?" asked Chef Gary.

"Sweet potato cream cheese with crushed candied pecans."

Chef Gary nodded. "Sweetness and crunch—good combination."

Tate was busy trying to concentrate on cooking. Trying to not think about his dad. It wasn't easy.

"Hello, Tate. What are you making?"

He looked up. "Oh." It was Chef Porter. He would have been happier to see Nancy the chicken.

He didn't feel like talking. He pointed to the oven. "Beets."

Chef Porter peered into the oven. "And then?"

Tate sighed. "It'll be a molten chocolate beet pudding cake."

"Pudding, chocolate, cake, and beets." Chef Porter tapped the table with her finger. "Interesting idea . . . Fine work." A second later she was gone.

It wasn't much of an interaction, but Tate didn't mind. He was alone again and nothing bad had happened.

CHAPTER 35

"Ten minutes left!" shouted Chef Gary.

No one was ready. No one was calm. Everyone was rushing.

Rae dropped three dollops of lime sauce onto the plate and swirled them with the back of her spoon. She placed her spiced tart opposite the swirls and stacked three brittle pieces on the edge. A sprinkling of coconut shavings and a sugar-coated candied poblano pepper finished off the presentation.

Tate's pudding was droopy—like someone had punched it right in the middle. It probably tasted good, but presentation-wise, he needed more than sugarcoated beet slices to save it. He quickly melted some chocolate in a double boiler and dribbled it onto wax paper. He moved back and forth, slow and steady, creating an even and intricate gridlike pattern. Now he just needed time. Once it was set, he could put all of the components together.

Caroline was building her masterpiece layer by layer.

First the puff pastry, then a layer of pastry cream followed by caramelized apple and eggplant slices, a sprinkling of ground pistachios, and then puff pastry again to start a new layer. The final layer was a puff pastry crust with a vanilla glaze accented with swirls of caramel sauce. Caroline squeezed three dots of caramel sauce on the plate and dusted ground pistachios selectively around the remaining white space.

Oliver was worried. His ice cream wasn't freezing fast enough. He'd scooped out a tigger melon and filled it with ice cream. Now he was waiting for it to freeze. The plan was to slice off a small wedge for presentation. Oliver ran to the freezer: ready or not, he had to use it. Two sweet potato fritters were already on the plate, stacked and glazed with a drizzle of lavender honey. Oliver held his breath and carefully sliced the melon. The ice cream held together in a perfect wedge. He balanced two wafer-thin potato crisps next to the melon. A sprig of mint finished off the presentation.

"Time!" called Chef Gary, and everyone's hands went into the air. A second later the cameras turned off.

"Which one first?" asked Steve.

Chef Nancy pointed to Oliver. Mark the cameraperson ran over and took some close-ups of Oliver's dessert. When he was done, Oliver took his dessert to the freezer.

It took about ten minutes to film everyone's food. When they were done, the cameras got back into position and everyone pretended there hadn't been a break.

"And, rolling!" called Steve.

The judges stood in front of the long table at the head of the room.

Chef Gary pointed to the table. "Rae, please bring your dessert to the table."

Rae held her breath the whole way. Dropping the plate was everyone's worst fear.

"What did you make us?" asked Chef Aimee.

"Spiced lime and mango tart with spicy poblano brittle."

She could hardly breathe. The judges were going to try *her* food. Right now! Right in front of her. She held the charm on her neck for luck. She felt dizzy, but not fainting dizzy. This was excitement dizzy.

"*OOOH OOOOOH!*" Chef Gary surprised her with a song. "See, I told you I would sing. I couldn't help it. It's *that* surprisingly delicious!"

"Nice spicy crust," said Chef Aimee. "And it contrasts perfectly with the sweetness of the mango."

"Mmm—and the brittle! Very nice texture," said Chef Porter, and she took another piece.

Rae went back to her spot in a daze—a happy daze.

Chef Gary pointed at the table. "Caroline, please bring your dessert to the table."

Caroline made it there without incident. That was lucky: her hands were sweaty and shaking.

"What did you make us?" asked Chef Aimee.

"Apple eggplant napoleon with pistachio dust and a vanilla caramel glaze."

Chef Aimee took the first bite. "Nice crunch on the puff pastry, and those mini eggplants are like candy. The bottom layer is a little soggy, but it tastes so good, I almost don't mind."

Chef Porter smiled. "Beautiful presentation and delicious pastry cream. Just perfect—not too sweet."

Chef Gary took the last and the biggest bite. "I want to sing your praises, but Chef Aimee won't let me do any more singing, so all I can say is . . . this is amazing!"

Caroline went back to her spot with a huge smile on her face.

"Ten-minute break!" shouted Steve. He pointed to Oliver's dessert. "And get that one back in the freezer."

Chef Nancy helped Oliver with his dessert, Caroline and Rae sat down to rest, and Tate ran off to the bathroom.

CHAPTER 36

en minutes later, everyone was back at their workstations except Tate. He was missing. Chef Nancy knew just where to look, and it wasn't the bathroom.

"Tate! We're about to start!"

Tate grumbled, said goodbye to his dad, and followed Chef Nancy back to the studio.

As soon as he was back at his workstation, things started up again.

"Cameras rolling!"

Chef Gary pointed at the table. "Tate, please bring your dessert to the table."

Tate moved faster than the others, and he didn't seem worried about dropping his plate.

"What did you make for us?" asked Chef Porter.

Tate couldn't believe his luck. He always got Chef Porter.

He answered without looking up. "Molten chocolate beet pudding cake with a chocolate web crust garnished with candied yellow and red beets."

"I do love beets," said Chef Porter. She tasted the pudding with her spoon. "Subtle, but I think it might need just a touch more sweetness."

Tate nodded. He was mad at himself. He'd made the most common cooking mistake ever. He'd forgotten to taste it before baking it.

Chef Gary took a bite, then scrunched up his nose. "I'm trying to taste the beets, but it's a little bland." He sucked on a candied beet and nodded. "But these are good."

Chef Aimee wasn't very excited about the taste either. "Tate, did you try this before you baked it?"

Tate stared at the table and shook his head.

"I'm sorry, Tate. It would certainly have made a difference, because the consistency is excellent."

It was a compliment, sort of. Tate looked up and tried to smile.

Then he looked back down, disappointed. His dessert was a failure. There was a good chance he'd be the one going home.

Chef Gary pointed to Oliver. "Oliver, will you please bring your dessert to the table."

Oliver walked up slowly and carefully. Any sudden

movements and the potato crisps would slip right off the plate.

"Oliver, what did you make us?"

"Chef, I made sweet potatoes three ways. Sweet potato fritters with a honey lavender glaze, sweet potato ice cream with pecans, and sweet potato maple crisps."

Chef Gary leaned forward for a closer look. "WOW! What a presentation. I don't think I've seen anything quite like this before. The orange ice cream in the orange melon—that's brilliant! It looks like it was meant to be that way." He dug his spoon into the ice cream. "Creamy, smooth, with just a little bite—delicious." He licked his lips.

Chef Aimee was next. Her favorites were the fritters and the ice cream. "What a satisfying combination, and the fritters are light and fluffy—not at all greasy. Excellent job, Oliver."

And last there was Chef Porter. She tried everything, closed her eyes, and then spoke only one word: "Bravo!"

The judges moved away from the table to talk about the desserts. It was hard to wait and do nothing. Rae counted by fives, Tate tapped his feet, Caroline scratched her arm, and Oliver tried to lip-read. The judges were talking, but of course he couldn't hear what they were saying. Lip-reading was harder than he thought it would be. He studied Chef Porter. Was she really saying *Aloha green bean*?

CHAPTER 37

he judges moved back to the center of the room. Chef Gary stepped forward. "We are proud of each and every one of you. You are the top junior chefs in the country and we are honored to have you in this competition. Today's challenge was not easy, and you did not disappoint us. The desserts you've presented are inspiring, creative, and daring.

"Rae, your sweet and spicy tart was a treat for our tongues.

"Caroline, your twist on the napoleon was unexpected and delightful.

"Oliver, your trio of desserts was beyond expectation.

"Tate, the pairing of chocolate and beets is brilliant.

This was a hard competition to judge, but the contestant we chose displayed an incredible amount of ingenuity and skill."

Rae would have never thought to put eggplants in a

napoleon—that was ingenious. Could Caroline be the winner?

Caroline studied Rae's dessert. She'd made both a tart and brittle—that was skillful. Could Rae be the winner?

Chef Gary put his hands on the table right next to Rae's dessert. "Not only was the dessert delicious, but it was also exquisitely presented."

Chef Gary waved his hand over the desserts. "Presentation is always important, and there are some nice examples of that here. Rae used brittle to add height, Tate added a chocolate grid for mystery, and Oliver's plate was filled

with sculptural elements. Caroline, I'm not leaving you out. Sometimes less is more, and that was the case for your napoleon. It's a multilayered dessert, complicated in its structure, so it deserves to be the standout on the plate. Well done."

Chef Gary stepped back to join the other judges.

Caroline held her breath.

Oliver stared without blinking.

Tate wiggled his toes.

Rae counted to ten.

Chef Gary nodded to the other judges. They smiled and nodded back. "The winner of today's elimination challenge is . . . Oliver!"

The whole room broke out in applause.

"I loved it," gushed Chef Aimee. "I can't believe you created three different incredible desserts in only ninety minutes. Oliver, we can't wait to see what you do next!"

Chef Porter stepped up. "Well done, young man. Very impressive!"

Oliver bowed and then bowed again and again—once for each chef. "Thank you, Chef! Thank you, Chef! Thank you,

Chef!" He couldn't stop smiling. This was it! The best day of his life.

Chef Gary invited Oliver over to stand next to him. He shook his hand. "As the winner of this challenge, we'd like to present you with this certificate for five hundred dollars' worth of new cooking supplies and maybe more importantly . . . an advantage in the next round."

Chef Gary stood back and watched as a table was wheeled over to the center of the room. There were three elements on the table: a flaming disk, a glass bowl filled with water, and a spinning pinwheel.

Chef Gary pointed to the table. "Fire, water, and air! One of these *might* be an advantage in the next round. Oliver, please think carefully, then make your choice."

Oliver nodded and started a countdown in his head. It looked like he was thinking, but really he'd already chosen. Fire! That was the advantage—he was sure of it. *Three, two, one.* He smiled. "I choose fire."

After the excitement with Oliver, there was one more task: elimination. No one was smiling for this part.

Chef Aimee looked sad. "I'm sorry. This is so hard, but we have to send someone home." She scanned the remaining contestants. "Rae, will you please step up."

Caroline gasped.

Rae's feet didn't want to move, but she willed them forward, closer to Chef Aimee. She stared at Chef Aimee's lips, waiting for the words. What would happen when they came? Would she cry? Yes! It was starting already.

The lips smiled. "Rae, you will not be eliminated today. Please join Oliver at the front."

Rae screamed and ran forward, then spun to look behind her. *Oh no! Not Caroline!*

Caroline was staring at the floor, her hands shaking at her sides.

Chef Aimee looked back and forth between Caroline and Tate. "You are both talented and deserving, but one of you will be asked to leave. Caroline, your dessert was inspired, but skill is also important. Your bottom crust was soggy and that detracted from the dessert. Tate, as you know, taste is just as important as presentation. Your dessert looked delicious, but lacked the follow-through. It was not sweet enough." Chef Aimee shook her head.

"Caroline . . . will you please step forward." Caroline stepped forward, then looked up. A large tear was wiggling a crooked path down her cheek.

"Caroline, you may join Oliver and Rae at the front."

Caroline sobbed in relief and stepped next to Oliver.

Chef Aimee walked over to Tate and patted his shoulder. "Tate, we've loved having you here in the *Next Best Junior Chef* competition. There are great things in store for you. I know we'll hear from you again. You are truly a talented young chef, but your dessert tonight was a bit of a disappointment. I'm afraid you are no longer in the running to be the Next Best Junior Chef. Please hang up your apron."

Tate was surprised, but not about losing. The surprise was how he felt. He wasn't one bit sad. He looked up at Chef Aimee and the other judges. "Thank you, chefs, for the opportunity. I had a lot of fun." He walked to his workstation and hung up his apron, and then he was gone, out the big back door.

Rae watched, sad for Tate but glad that it wasn't her. This wasn't goodbye; they'd see him later, back at the lodge. He still had to pack up his things. It helped that she knew where he was right at that minute—probably hugging his dad.

TATE

I really had fun in the competition. I learned a lot and made some great friends. I don't feel like I lost, because having my dad here is better than winning the competition. It's better than any prize I could have ever imagined!

Caroline looked over at Oliver. He was smiling, but was he sad, too? His buddy was leaving. Caroline wanted to be next to Rae, so they could hold hands. Competing against your new best friend wasn't easy, and it certainly wasn't natural. Friends needed to stick together. How could they do that now? Team up against Oliver?

CHAPTER 38

C hef Aimee clapped her hands and admired the three remaining contestants. "Are you ready for the next round of challenges? I hope so, because it's going to be exciting!"

"YES, CHEF!"

Caroline's mouth said the words, but she was worried.

What have you learned that will help you win Next Best Junior Chef?

I've learned that food is like friendship: the more you're around it, the better you understand it.

RAE

OLIVER

I've learned that calmness is a skill, not just a title. I'm going to work to live up to my name. I'll be the King of Calm in life and in the kitchen.

I've learned to listen to myself, and be confident in my decisions. I have hidden skills that I'm just discovering.

CAROLINE

"Congratulations, contestants. You are moving on to the next round of *Next Best Junior Chef*! What new challenges will test our young chefs' culinary skills? What unexpected hurdles will be thrown in their path? Will the bonds of friendship survive? Who will be eliminated next? And who will be one dish closer to winning the competition? Tune in to the next episode of *Next Best Junior Chef* to find out!"

STAY TUNED FOR SCENES FROM EPISODE 2 OF NEXT BEST JUNIOR CHEF!

Essential Knife Techniques for the Young Chef

from *The Young Chef: Recipes and Techniques for Kids Who Love to Cook* by the Culinary Institute of America

· ·

These techniques are the cornerstone of every chef's success. The better practiced you are at these methods, the better a chef you will become—and the better your food will look and taste.

Knife Skills

A chef's skill with a knife helps him or her work quickly and efficiently with accuracy. Precise and uniform knife cuts are one of the keys to beautiful-looking food.

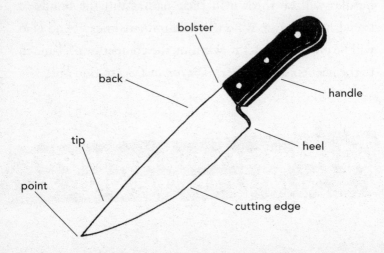

Knife Safety

Understanding how to use and maintain knives and other kitchen tools is an important part of working in the kitchen and essential to your own safety. You may need to talk to your parents before using kitchen knives. Here are some important rules:

- Keep knives sharp. A dull knife can be dangerous and make you more likely to cut yourself.
- Keep knives clean and dry. Dirty knives can cause cross-contamination.
- Store knives in a knife block, on a magnetic strip, or in a drawer with plastic knife sheaths so that they are stable and the blades are protected.
- Use the right knife for the job.
- Never put knives into a sink full of water. They can be hidden and could cut someone who reaches into the water.
- Make sure your cutting board is stable and not hanging over the edge of the counter. You can secure a cutting board on the counter by putting a wet paper towel underneath.
- Never pass a knife to someone; always lay it safely on the counter to be picked up.

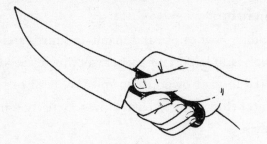

Handling a Chef's Knife

Your hand should be placed at the point where the blade and the handle meet. Angle your fingers down and make sure your thumb is tucked in behind your index finger.

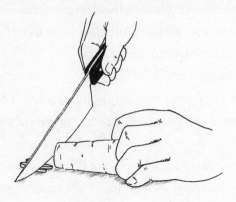

Hold the food with a clawlike grip. Cut the food with even knife strokes from the tip to the heel of the knife. Move the hand that is holding the food in place back little by little as you cut back along the food.

Three Common Knife Cuts

Slicing

Cutting in a straight downward motion at regular intervals so that pieces are uniform in size.

Julienning

Cutting into long, uniform "sticks" (pictured above). Accomplished by first squaring off the sides of the vegetable to make a rectangle. The "block" is cut lengthwise into slices, and then the slices are stacked neatly and cut into sticks.

Dicing

Cutting into uniform cubes. After cutting into julienne sticks, gather sticks and cut them crosswise into small cubes.

Foods can be diced into large (¾ inch), medium (about ⅓ inch), or small (¼ inch) pieces, or very tiny (⅛) pieces, which chefs call brunoise.

AND NOW A SNEAK PEEK AT EPISODE 2 OF *NEXT BEST JUNIOR CHEF!*

NEXT BEST JUNIOR CHEF

EPISODE 2

THE HEAT IS ON

Cotton Candy

"mezzaluna"

spicy!

by Charise Mericle Harper

THE HEAT IS ON

"PLACES, EVERYONE!" Steve held up his hand. "And cameras . . . rolling!"

Chef Gary stood at the front of the room. "You'll have five minutes in the pantry and then we'll start cooking, but remember, if you've forgotten anything *you can* go back. Your time starts . . . NOW!"

Caroline, Oliver, and Rae grabbed their baskets and raced into the pantry. Rae recited the five ingredients from the top of her list: "Anchovy paste, soy sauce, tomato paste, fish sauce, and olive oil." No one cared that she talked to herself—they were used to it. Ten minutes ago she'd been desperate, but now she was on a mission. "Umami paste to the rescue!"

"TIME!" shouted Chef Aimee.

Everyone raced back to their workstations.

A minute later, Chef Aimee gave the official start. "LET'S GET COOKING!"

The camerapeople moved in for a close-up of Oliver's workstation. His first step was *mise en place*—that was French for "everything in its place." Everything needed to be chopped, measured, and portioned into bowls before he even started cooking. The benefits were huge—less chance of making a mistake, and faster access to the ingredients.

Caroline grabbed her potatoes and started peeling. There was a lot to do.

Chef Aimee came by just as she began grating. "Oh dear, are you okay?"

Tears steamed down Caroline's face. She nodded. "It's the onions, but I'm almost done." She dumped the grated potatoes and onions in a dishtowel and moved over to the sink. "I need to wring these out and get them as dry as possible, because extra moisture will make my potato cups soggy."

"Clever," said Chef Aimee. "I'm impressed."

Caroline blushed.

CAROLINE

I'm cooking my hot dog in the oven. I don't want it to dry out, so I'll put it in a baking dish with just a little beef consommé and roast it at around 400 degrees for ten to twelve minutes. The consommé will help it stay moist, and the baking will make it perfectly brown.

Rae was waiting for Chef Aimee when she arrived. She held up a mason jar. "Pickled onions. I made them right away, so the onions would have time to absorb the flavor of the vinegar." She dipped a spoon into her bowl and stirred. "And now I'm making an umami paste."

Chef Aimee leaned over the bowl to look. "What's in it?"

Rae rattled off a list of ingredients, and then stopped. "Oh no! I forgot the Parmesan cheese."

Chef Aimee pointed to the pantry. "Well, don't waste time talking to me."

Rae gave a fast wave and ran off. When she came back Chef Aimee was gone. Too bad—she'd wanted to tell her about her potato salad. Hopefully no one else was using sweet potatoes. Rae grabbed the Parmesan cheese and quickly grated it into the bowl. The potatoes were next, and if they weren't peeled and boiling in the next five minutes she'd be in trouble. She sighed. This was definitely going to be a race, up until the very last minute.

I'm going boil my hot dog, but not just in water. I'll add salt, vinegar, cumin, and nutmeg. After five minutes in a simmering bath, it'll be perfect.

RAE

Oliver was Chef Aimee's last stop. His countertop was filled with bowls, tools, cutting boards, pots, pans, and Oliver was racing back and forth.

Chef Aimee watched, shaking her head. "Oliver, what's going on here? This isn't how you usually work. It looks . . . kind of crazy."

Oliver nodded. "Yes, ma'am. I know, but there's so much to do."

Chef Aimee put her hand on his shoulder. "Let's take a breather, just for a minute. Take me through your process."

Oliver pointed to each bowl and identified them. "Bowl one is sriracha barbecue sauce—still needs paprika and Worcestershire sauce. Bowl two: sauce to add to the red onion marmalade once the onions are done cooking. Bowl three: homemade ketchup—I'll add this finishing sauce once I've blended the tomatoes, onions, vinegar, water, and sugar in the food processor." Oliver fidgeted and pointed to a stack of potatoes. "I'm sorry, ma'am. I really need to get to those if I'm going to finish my rosti on time."

Chef Aimee raised her arms and stepped back. "Of course, Oliver, continue. I don't know how you did it, but it looks like you've got this under control."

OLIVER

I've scored my hot dog and am marinating it in a mixture of oil, homemade ketchup, soy sauce, and garlic. It'll absorb these flavors and the moisture from the sauce. When I put it in the pan, it will steam on the inside and grill on the outside. It's the best way to make a perfectly cooked hot dog. And I'll use bacon fat instead of butter.

"Thirty minutes," called Chef Gary.

"No!" Caroline banged a spatula on the table.

Chef Gary rushed over to check on her.

"Ugh!" She dropped the spatula and picked up a fork. The mini potato cups were sticking to the muffin tin.

Chef Gary stepped up and sniffed. "Mmm, smells good. Might be worth the trouble to get them out."

Caroline smiled halfheartedly and attacked the tin again. This time the plump potato cup popped right out. She picked up a bowl started mixing.

Chef Gary watched. "What's that?"

"Homemade ranch dressing."

He covered his mouth. "I'd better go before I start drooling."

"Eye on the clock! FIFTEEN MINUTES LEFT!" Chef Aimee clapped her hands.

That was just enough time for the last two visits—Rae and Oliver.

Chef Gary picked a skewer off Rae's table and twirled it. "I think we've seen these recently."

"Yes Chef, but with a new recipe. I'm making potato salad on a stick . . . with sweet potatoes." She dropped a quarter cup of diced poblano chiles into her bowl of potato chunks. "I have to mix these in carefully—I don't want to smash my potatoes." She picked up a wooden spoon and carefully folded the ingredients together.

Chef Gary returned the skewer. "Good work, Rae! I can't wait to try that flavor combination."

"Sweet and spicy to go with umami!" Rae looked up to smile at Chef Gary, but he was already heading off to see Oliver.

Oliver was shaking his head and his frying pan.

"What's cooking?" asked Chef Gary.

"Not this potato rosti!" snapped Oliver. Then he quickly apologized. "I'm sorry, sir, but it's these potatoes. I want crispy, not soggy."

"Creative problem-solving." Chef Gary tapped his head. "Take a minute and think it through."

Oliver nodded, took a deep breath, and studied his pan. Suddenly, he knew what to do. "Thank you, Chef!" His pan was too crowded. The rosti was steaming not frying. He sliced the rosti into eight and pulled out four pie-shaped wedges. A minute later, four remaining slices were back on the stove, crisping up.

Chef Gary walked to the center of the room. "FIVE MINUTES!"

"AHHH!" Rae drizzled five droplets of poblano honey dressing on the side of the plate.

Oliver cut three thin wedges of potato rosti and balanced them on edge next to a small ramekin of ketchup.

Caroline stacked three mini potato cups one on top of another and was just about to add a last decorative sprig of cilantro when . . .

"TIME! HANDS UP!"

"CUT!" yelled Steve.

To be continued . . .